A LUCKY LUKE ADVENTURE

THE STAGECOACH

BY MORRIS & GOSCINNY

9th CINEBOOK
The 9th Art Publisher

BLACK BART (Charles E. Bolton)
The ghost/poet/robber of stagecoaches who signed off his attacks by leaving poems he'd written in the empty safes. Here is a sample of his strange lyrical talent:

I've labored long and hard for bread,
For honor and for riches,
But on my corns too long you've tred,
You fine-haired sons of b…

Black Bart the Po-8

Original title: Lucky Luke – La diligence
Original edition: © Dargaud Editeur Paris 1968 by Goscinny and Morris
© Lucky Comics
www.lucky-luke.com
English translation: © 2010 Cinebook Ltd
Translator: Luke Spear
Lettering and text layout: Imadjinn sarl
Printed in Spain by Just Colour Graphic
This edition published in Great Britain in 2010 by
Cinebook Ltd
56 Beech Avenue
Canterbury, Kent
CT4 7TA
www.cinebook.com
A CIP catalogue record for this book
is available from the British Library
ISBN 978-1-84918-052-8

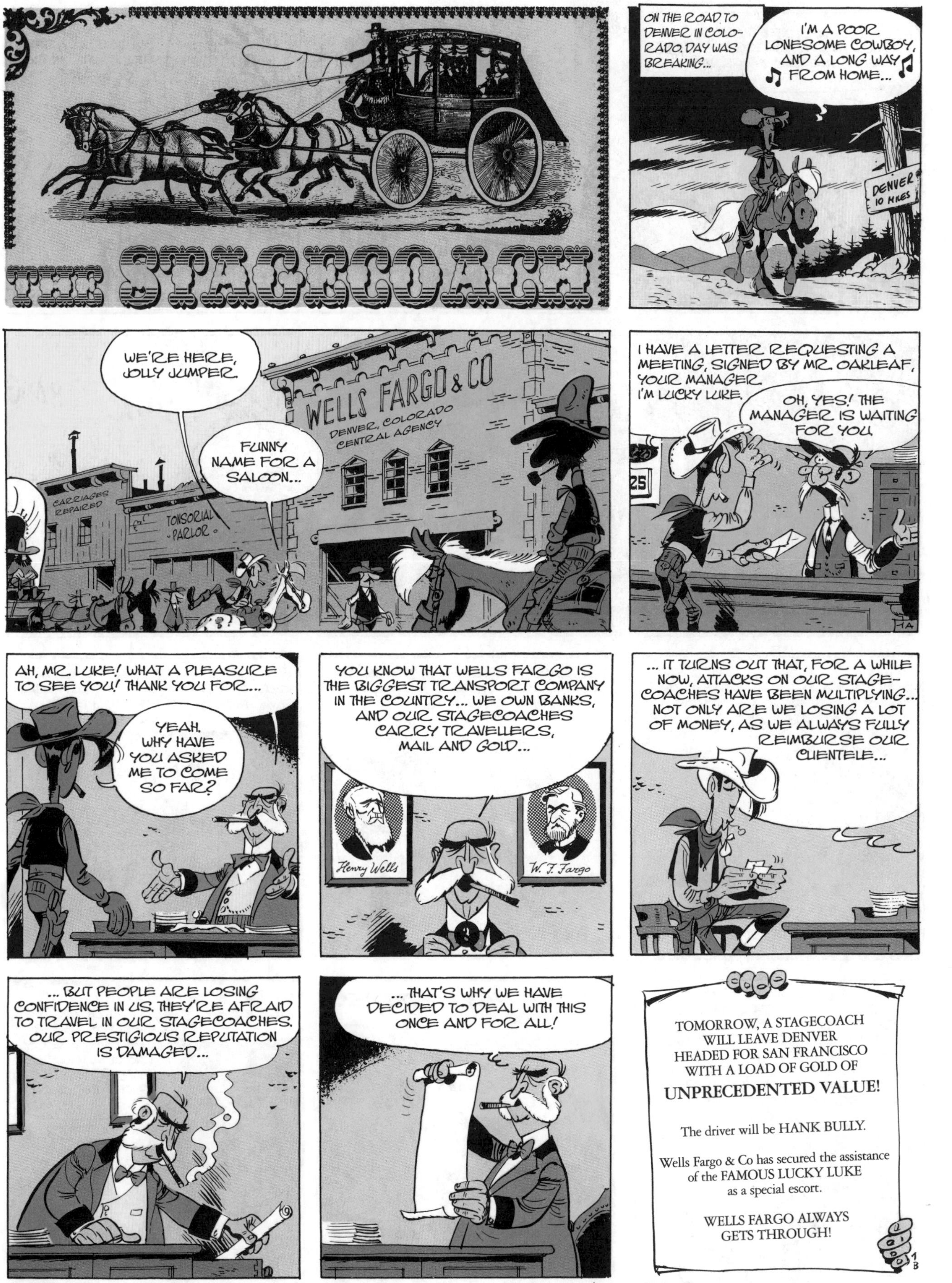
THE STAGECOACH
ON THE ROAD TO DENVER IN COLORADO. DAY WAS BREAKING...
I'M A POOR LONESOME COWBOY, AND A LONG WAY FROM HOME...
DENVER 10 MILES
WE'RE HERE, JOLLY JUMPER.
WELLS FARGO & CO
DENVER, COLORADO CENTRAL AGENCY
CARRIAGES REPAIRED
TONSORIAL PARLOR
FUNNY NAME FOR A SALOON...
I HAVE A LETTER REQUESTING A MEETING, SIGNED BY MR. OARLEAF, YOUR MANAGER. I'M LUCKY LUKE.
OH, YES! THE MANAGER IS WAITING FOR YOU.
AH, MR. LUKE! WHAT A PLEASURE TO SEE YOU! THANK YOU FOR...
YEAH. WHY HAVE YOU ASKED ME TO COME SO FAR?
YOU KNOW THAT WELLS FARGO IS THE BIGGEST TRANSPORT COMPANY IN THE COUNTRY... WE OWN BANKS, AND OUR STAGECOACHES CARRY TRAVELLERS, MAIL AND GOLD...
Henry Wells
W. F. Fargo
... IT TURNS OUT THAT, FOR A WHILE NOW, ATTACKS ON OUR STAGECOACHES HAVE BEEN MULTIPLYING... NOT ONLY ARE WE LOSING A LOT OF MONEY, AS WE ALWAYS FULLY REIMBURSE OUR CLIENTELE...
... BUT PEOPLE ARE LOSING CONFIDENCE IN US. THEY'RE AFRAID TO TRAVEL IN OUR STAGECOACHES. OUR PRESTIGIOUS REPUTATION IS DAMAGED...
... THAT'S WHY WE HAVE DECIDED TO DEAL WITH THIS ONCE AND FOR ALL!
TOMORROW, A STAGECOACH WILL LEAVE DENVER HEADED FOR SAN FRANCISCO WITH A LOAD OF GOLD OF
UNPRECEDENTED VALUE!
The driver will be HANK BULLY.
Wells Fargo & Co has secured the assistance of the FAMOUS LUCKY LUKE as a special escort.
WELLS FARGO ALWAYS GETS THROUGH!

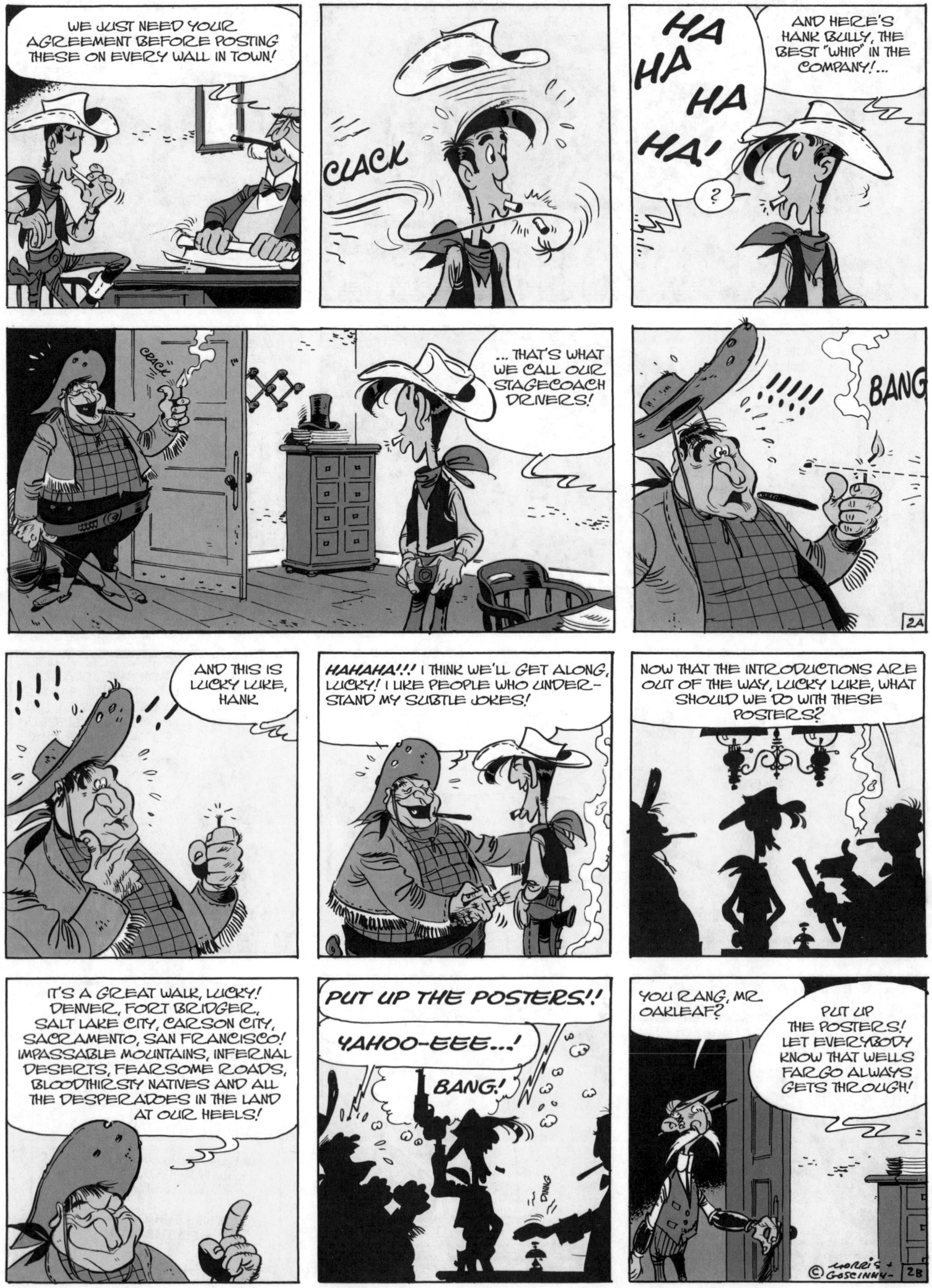
WE JUST NEED YOUR AGREEMENT BEFORE POSTING THESE ON EVERY WALL IN TOWN!
CLACK
HA HA HA HA!
AND HERE'S HANK BULLY, THE BEST "WHIP" IN THE COMPANY!...
?
CRACK
... THAT'S WHAT WE CALL OUR STAGECOACH DRIVERS!
!!!!!!
BANG
2A
!!!
AND THIS IS LUCKY LUKE, HANK
HAHAHA!!! I THINK WE'LL GET ALONG, LUCKY! I LIKE PEOPLE WHO UNDERSTAND MY SUBTLE JOKES!
NOW THAT THE INTRODUCTIONS ARE OUT OF THE WAY, LUCKY LUKE, WHAT SHOULD WE DO WITH THESE POSTERS?
IT'S A GREAT WALK, LUCKY! DENVER, FORT BRIDGER, SALT LAKE CITY, CARSON CITY, SACRAMENTO, SAN FRANCISCO! IMPASSABLE MOUNTAINS, INFERNAL DESERTS, FEARSOME ROADS, BLOODTHIRSTY NATIVES AND ALL THE DESPERADOES IN THE LAND AT OUR HEELS!
PUT UP THE POSTERS!!
YAHOO-EEE...!
BANG!
DING
YOU RANG, MR OAKLEAF?
PUT UP THE POSTERS! LET EVERYBODY KNOW THAT WELLS FARGO ALWAYS GETS THROUGH!
© MORRIS + GOSCINNY
2B

I'LL PREPARE YOUR CONTRACT, MR. LUKE. WE LEAVE TOMORROW MORNING.

LET'S DRINK TO THAT IN THE SALOON!

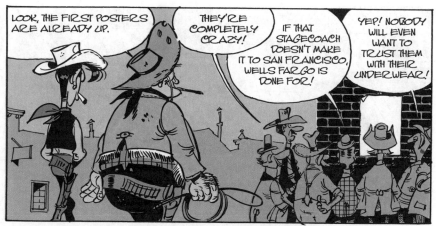

LOOK, THE FIRST POSTERS ARE ALREADY UP.

THEY'RE COMPLETELY CRAZY!

IF THAT STAGECOACH DOESN'T MAKE IT TO SAN FRANCISCO, WELLS FARGO IS DONE FOR!

YEP! NOBODY WILL EVEN WANT TO TRUST THEM WITH THEIR UNDERWEAR!

DARN IT! I'M USING THE WRONG DECK FOR PATIENCE...

CAT THUMBS!! YOU OLD DOG! THEY STILL HAVEN'T HANGED YOU YET?!

KEEP THE NOISE DOWN, HANK! NOBODY KNOWS ME IN THIS TOWN. I'VE JUST GOTTEN HERE, AND I HOPE TO FIND MYSELF SOME COMPETITION FOR POKER.

THEY'D HAVE TO BE ONE HECK OF A SUCKER TO AGREE TO PLAY WITH YOU!

NO MORE OF A SUCKER THAN YOU WITH YOUR NEXT JOURNEY... I'M TRYING TO WAGER 20 TO 1 THAT YOU WON'T MAKE IT TO SAN FRANCISCO, BUT I CAN'T FIND ANY TAKERS!

TIRED OF LIVING, HANK?... DARN IT, ANOTHER ACE!

CAT IS A PROFESSIONAL CHEAT, BUT WHEN HE'S NOT PLAYING, HE'S GREAT COMPANY!

TWO GLASSES OF ROTGUT!

ERM... HANK... WOULD YOU MIND SETTLING YOUR LITTLE TAB BEFORE LEAVING?...

THE LOCALS 'ROUND HERE AIN'T SO OPTIMISTIC!... I'M GOING TO BED. SEE YOU TOMORROW!

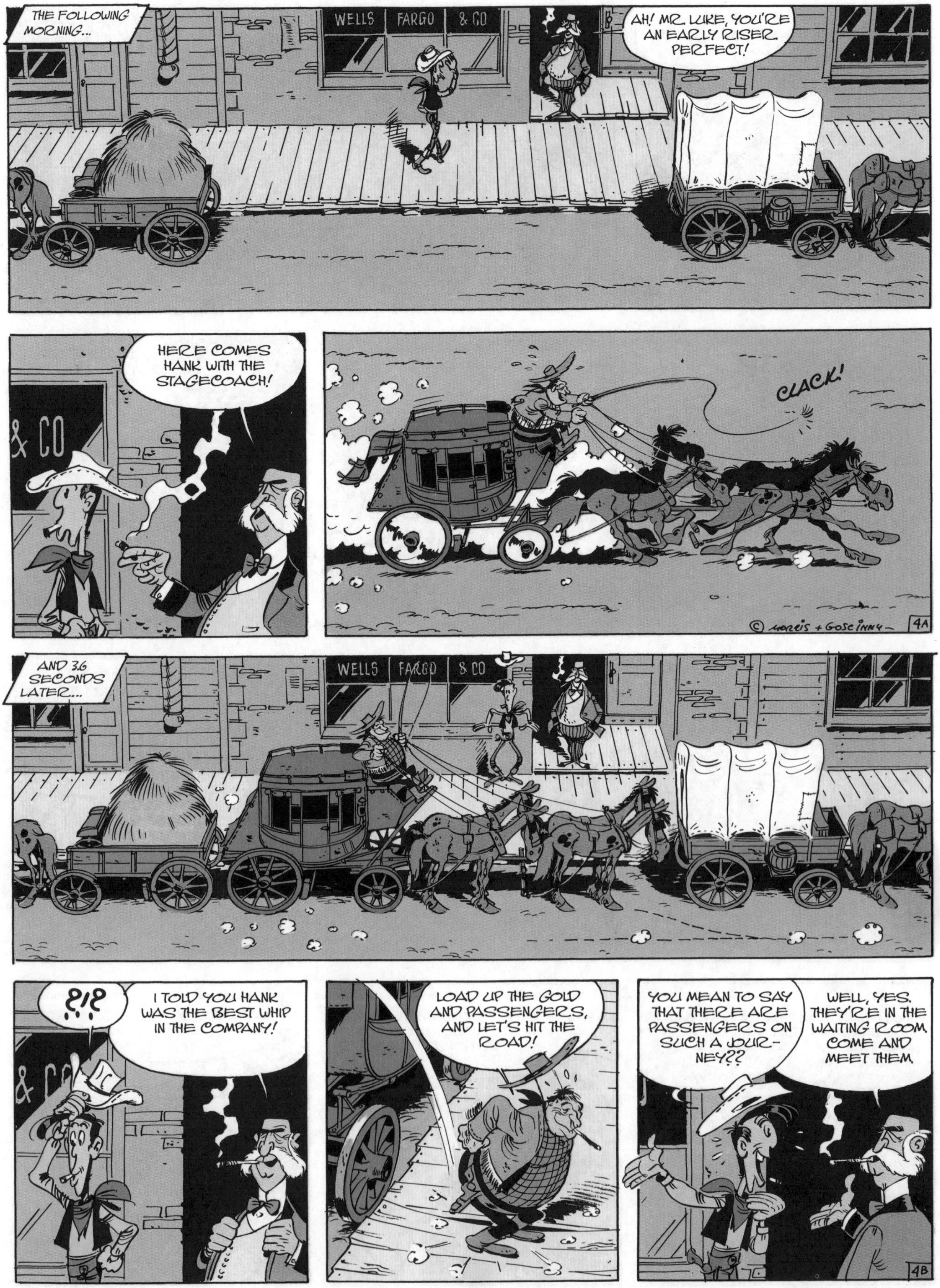

THE FOLLOWING MORNING...
WELLS FARGO & CO
AH! MR. LUKE, YOU'RE AN EARLY RISER. PERFECT!
& CO
HERE COMES HANK WITH THE STAGECOACH!
CLACK!
© MORRIS + GOSCINNY
4A
AND 3.6 SECONDS LATER...
WELLS FARGO & CO
?!?
I TOLD YOU HANK WAS THE BEST WHIP IN THE COMPANY!
LOAD UP THE GOLD AND PASSENGERS, AND LET'S HIT THE ROAD!
YOU MEAN TO SAY THAT THERE ARE PASSENGERS ON SUCH A JOURNEY??
WELL, YES. THEY'RE IN THE WAITING ROOM. COME AND MEET THEM.
4B

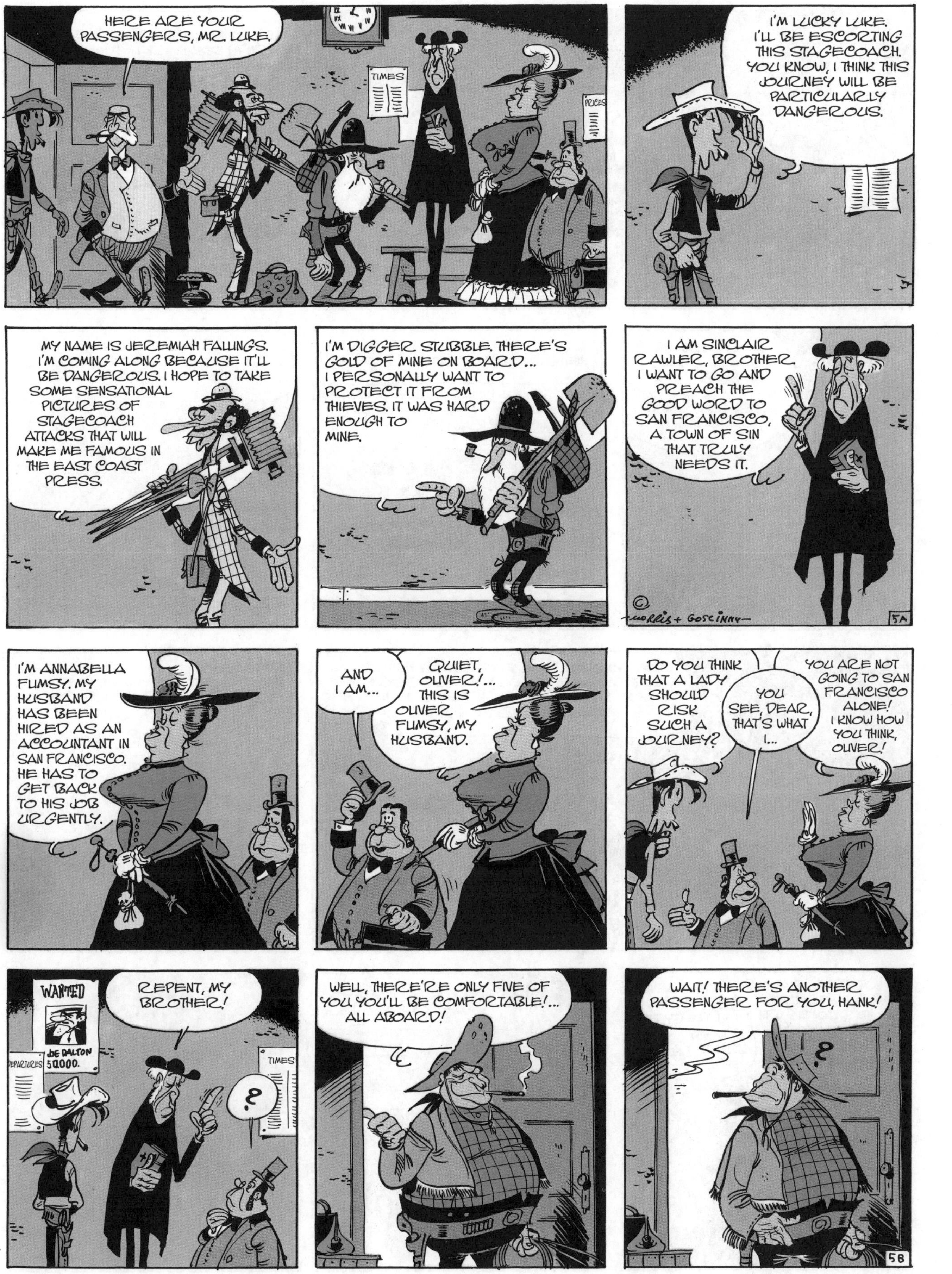
HERE ARE YOUR PASSENGERS, MR. LUKE.
TIMES
PRICES
I'M LUCKY LUKE. I'LL BE ESCORTING THIS STAGECOACH. YOU KNOW, I THINK THIS JOURNEY WILL BE PARTICULARLY DANGEROUS.
MY NAME IS JEREMIAH FALLINGS. I'M COMING ALONG BECAUSE IT'LL BE DANGEROUS. I HOPE TO TAKE SOME SENSATIONAL PICTURES OF STAGECOACH ATTACKS THAT WILL MAKE ME FAMOUS IN THE EAST COAST PRESS.
I'M DIGGER STUBBLE. THERE'S GOLD OF MINE ON BOARD... I PERSONALLY WANT TO PROTECT IT FROM THIEVES. IT WAS HARD ENOUGH TO MINE.
I AM SINCLAIR RAWLER, BROTHER. I WANT TO GO AND PREACH THE GOOD WORD TO SAN FRANCISCO, A TOWN OF SIN THAT TRULY NEEDS IT.
© MORRIS + GOSCINNY
5A
I'M ANNABELLA FUMSY. MY HUSBAND HAS BEEN HIRED AS AN ACCOUNTANT IN SAN FRANCISCO. HE HAS TO GET BACK TO HIS JOB URGENTLY.
AND I AM...
QUIET, OLIVER!... THIS IS OLIVER FUMSY, MY HUSBAND.
DO YOU THINK THAT A LADY SHOULD RISK SUCH A JOURNEY?
YOU SEE, DEAR, THAT'S WHAT I...
YOU ARE NOT GOING TO SAN FRANCISCO ALONE! I KNOW HOW YOU THINK, OLIVER!
WANTED
JOE DALTON 50000.
DEPARTURES
TIMES
REPENT, MY BROTHER!
?
WELL, THERE'RE ONLY FIVE OF YOU. YOU'LL BE COMFORTABLE!... ALL ABOARD!
WAIT! THERE'S ANOTHER PASSENGER FOR YOU, HANK!
?
58

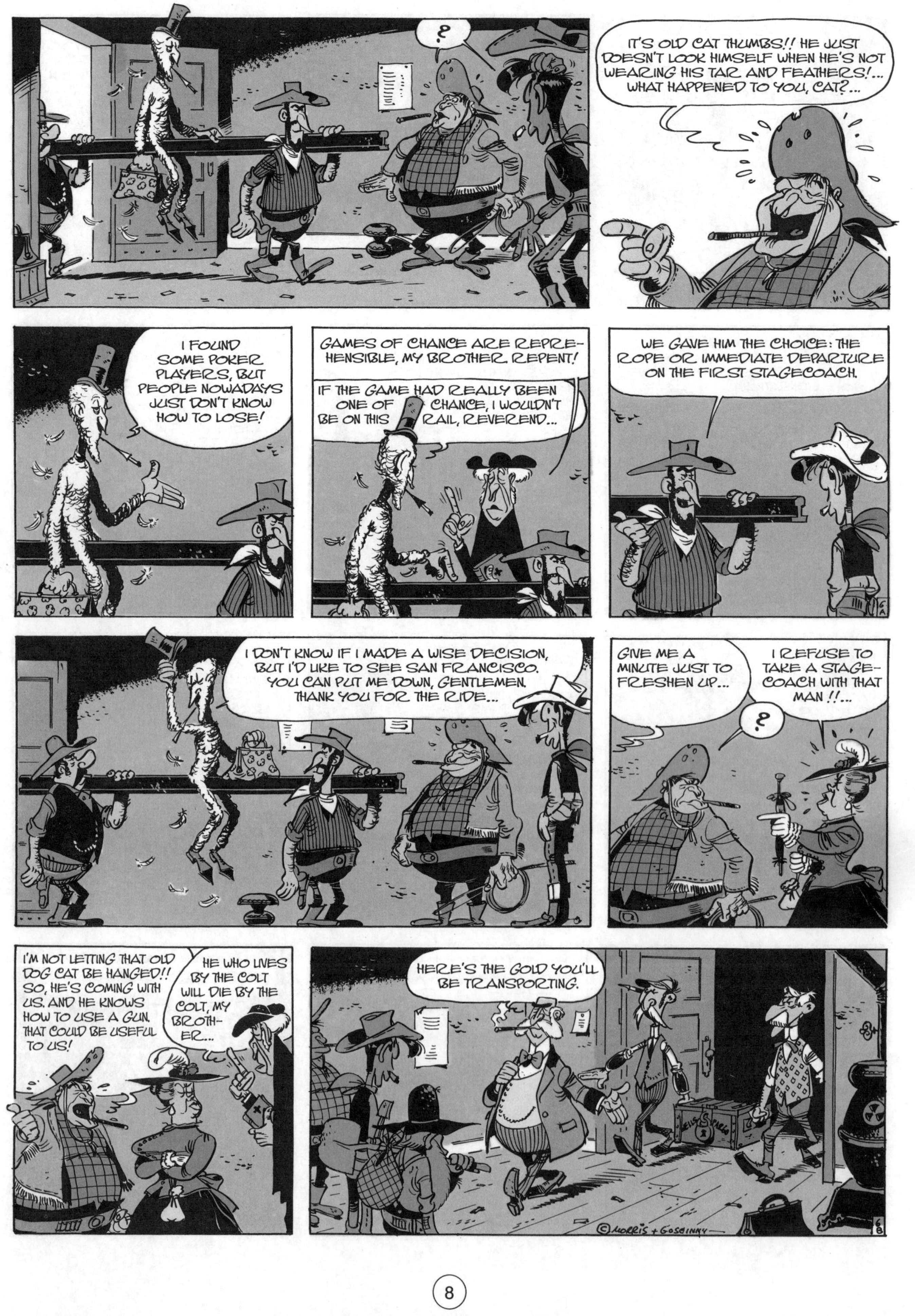
?
IT'S OLD CAT THUMBS!! HE JUST DOESN'T LOOK HIMSELF WHEN HE'S NOT WEARING HIS TAR AND FEATHERS!... WHAT HAPPENED TO YOU, CAT?...
I FOUND SOME POKER PLAYERS, BUT PEOPLE NOWADAYS JUST DON'T KNOW HOW TO LOSE!
GAMES OF CHANCE ARE REPREHENSIBLE, MY BROTHER. REPENT!
IF THE GAME HAD REALLY BEEN ONE OF CHANCE, I WOULDN'T BE ON THIS RAIL, REVEREND...
WE GAVE HIM THE CHOICE: THE ROPE OR IMMEDIATE DEPARTURE ON THE FIRST STAGECOACH.
I DON'T KNOW IF I MADE A WISE DECISION, BUT I'D LIKE TO SEE SAN FRANCISCO. YOU CAN PUT ME DOWN, GENTLEMEN. THANK YOU FOR THE RIDE...
GIVE ME A MINUTE JUST TO FRESHEN UP...
?
I REFUSE TO TAKE A STAGECOACH WITH THAT MAN!!...
I'M NOT LETTING THAT OLD DOG CAT BE HANGED!! SO, HE'S COMING WITH US. AND HE KNOWS HOW TO USE A GUN. THAT COULD BE USEFUL TO US!
HE WHO LIVES BY THE COLT WILL DIE BY THE COLT, MY BROTHER...
HERE'S THE GOLD YOU'LL BE TRANSPORTING.
WELLS FARGO
©MORRIS + GOSCINNY

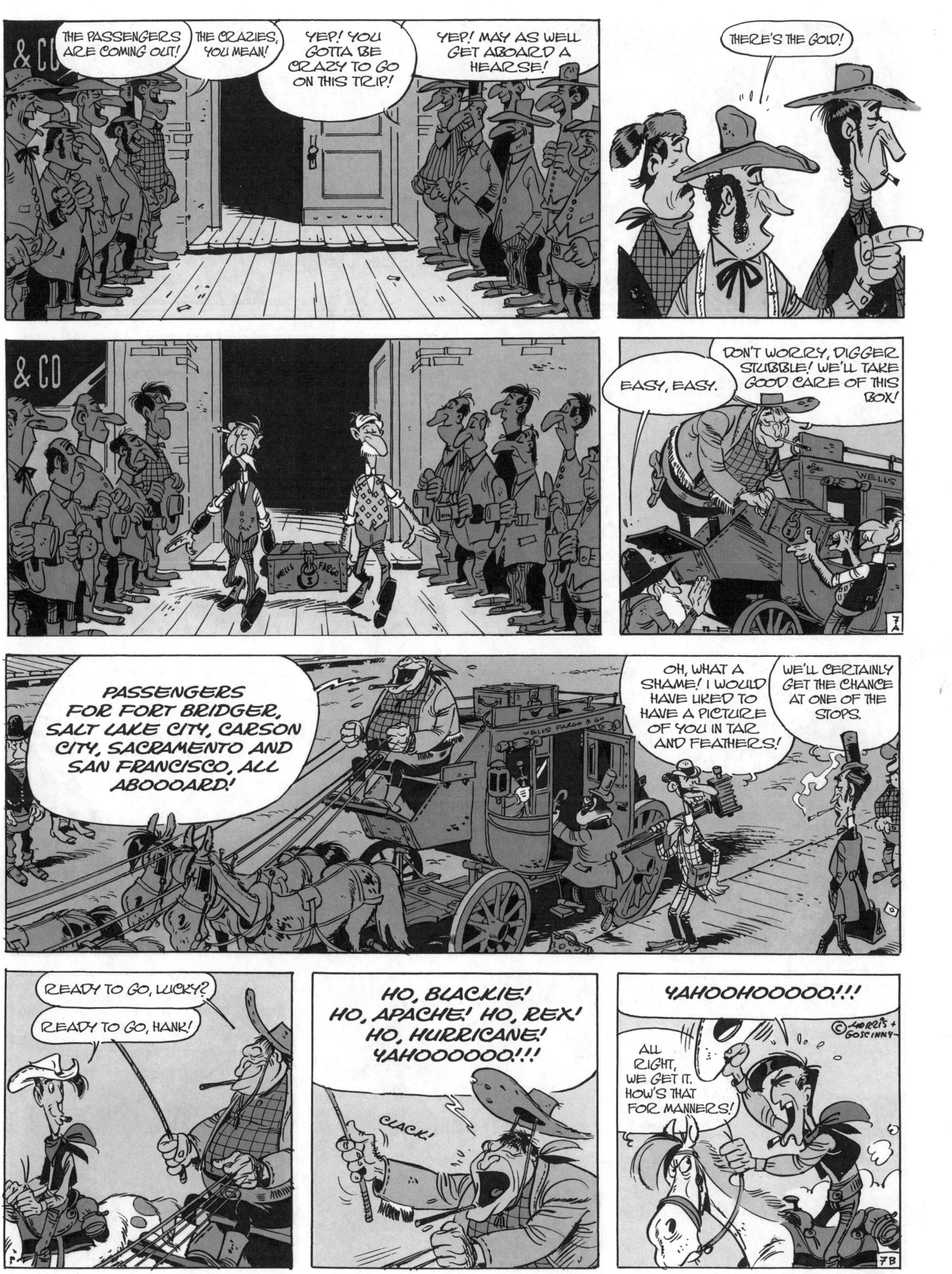
THE PASSENGERS ARE COMING OUT!
THE CRAZIES, YOU MEAN!
YEP! YOU GOTTA BE CRAZY TO GO ON THIS TRIP!
YEP! MAY AS WELL GET ABOARD A HEARSE!
THERE'S THE GOLD!
& CO
WELLS FARGO
EASY, EASY.
DON'T WORRY, DIGGER STUBBLE! WE'LL TAKE GOOD CARE OF THIS BOX!
WELLS
7A
PASSENGERS FOR FORT BRIDGER, SALT LAKE CITY, CARSON CITY, SACRAMENTO AND SAN FRANCISCO, ALL ABOOOARD!
WELLS FARGO & CO
OH, WHAT A SHAME! I WOULD HAVE LIKED TO HAVE A PICTURE OF YOU IN TAR AND FEATHERS!
WE'LL CERTAINLY GET THE CHANCE AT ONE OF THE STOPS.
READY TO GO, LUCKY?
READY TO GO, HANK!
HO, BLACKIE! HO, APACHE! HO, REX! HO, HURRICANE! YAHOOOOOO!!!
CLACK!
YAHOOHOOOOO!!!
© MORRIS + GOSCINNY
ALL RIGHT, WE GET IT. HOW'S THAT FOR MANNERS!
7B

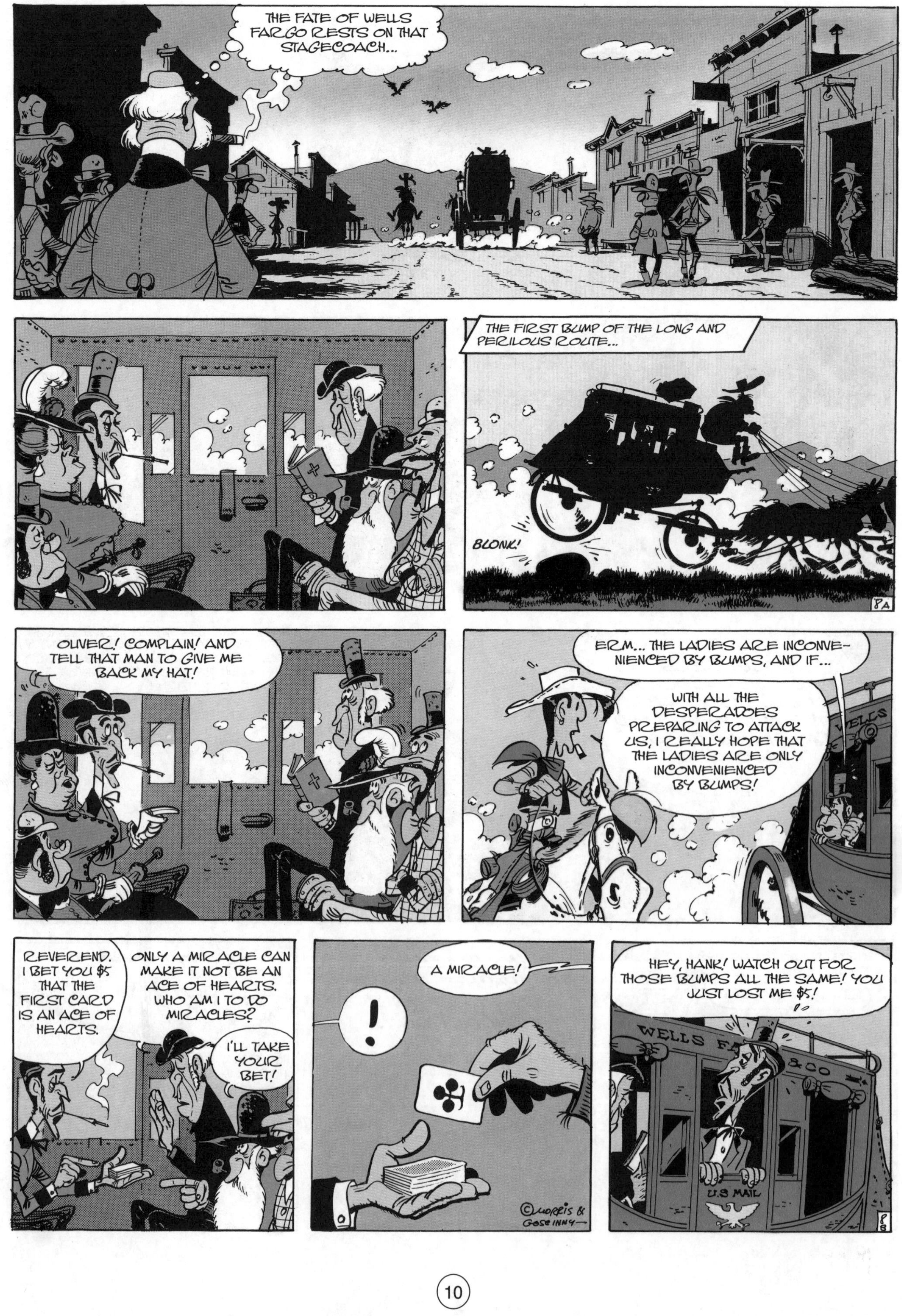
THE FATE OF WELLS FARGO RESTS ON THAT STAGECOACH...
THE FIRST BUMP OF THE LONG AND PERILOUS ROUTE...
BLONK!
OLIVER! COMPLAIN! AND TELL THAT MAN TO GIVE ME BACK MY HAT!
ERM... THE LADIES ARE INCONVE-NIENCED BY BUMPS, AND IF...
WITH ALL THE DESPERADOES PREPARING TO ATTACK US, I REALLY HOPE THAT THE LADIES ARE ONLY INCONVENIENCED BY BUMPS!
WELLS
REVEREND. I BET YOU $5 THAT THE FIRST CARD IS AN ACE OF HEARTS.
ONLY A MIRACLE CAN MAKE IT NOT BE AN ACE OF HEARTS. WHO AM I TO DO MIRACLES?
I'LL TAKE YOUR BET!
A MIRACLE!
!
©MORRIS & GOSCINNY
HEY, HANK! WATCH OUT FOR THOSE BUMPS ALL THE SAME! YOU JUST LOST ME $5!
WELLS FA
& CO
U.S MAIL

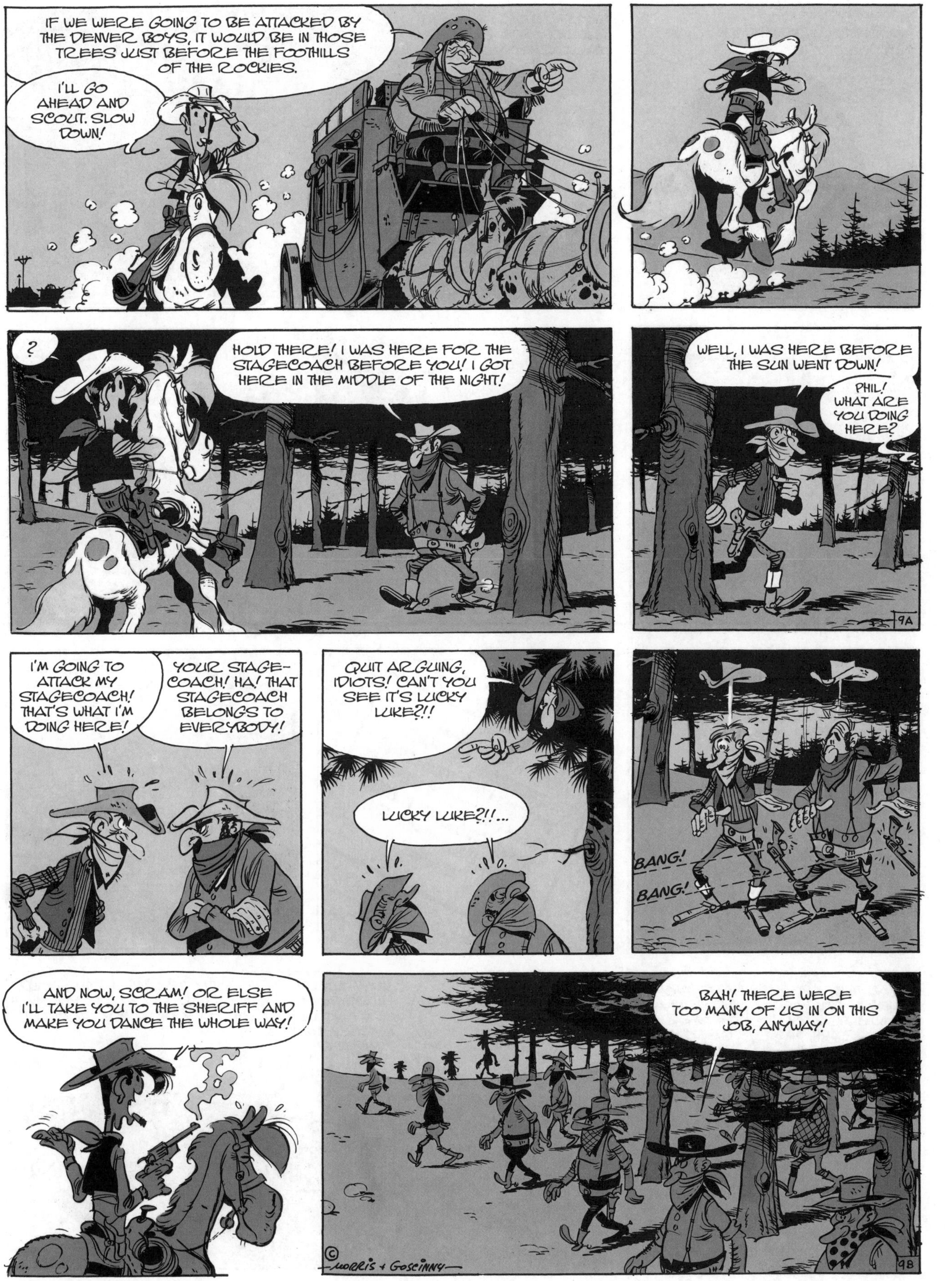

IF WE WERE GOING TO BE ATTACKED BY THE DENVER BOYS, IT WOULD BE IN THOSE TREES JUST BEFORE THE FOOTHILLS OF THE ROCKIES.
I'LL GO AHEAD AND SCOUT. SLOW DOWN!
?
HOLD THERE! I WAS HERE FOR THE STAGECOACH BEFORE YOU! I GOT HERE IN THE MIDDLE OF THE NIGHT!
WELL, I WAS HERE BEFORE THE SUN WENT DOWN!
PHIL! WHAT ARE YOU DOING HERE?
9A
I'M GOING TO ATTACK MY STAGECOACH! THAT'S WHAT I'M DOING HERE!
YOUR STAGE-COACH! HA! THAT STAGECOACH BELONGS TO EVERYBODY!
QUIT ARGUING, IDIOTS! CAN'T YOU SEE IT'S LUCKY LUKE?!!
LUCKY LUKE?!!...
BANG!
BANG!
AND NOW, SCRAM! OR ELSE I'LL TAKE YOU TO THE SHERIFF AND MAKE YOU DANCE THE WHOLE WAY!
BAH! THERE WERE TOO MANY OF US IN ON THIS JOB, ANYWAY!
© MORRIS + GOSCINNY
9B

OH? WHO COULD THIS BE NOW?...

BANG!

HMM?...

THE... THE STAGECOACH?

GONE!

ALWAYS THE SAME THING! EVERY TIME I LIE IN WAIT, I FALL ASLEEP! EVEN IF I DRINK COFFEE AND READ A PAPER TO STAY AWAKE, I FALL ASLEEP!

10A

!! !!!

© MORRIS + GOSCINNY

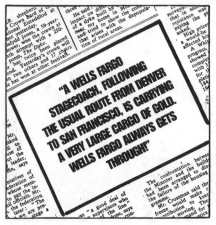

"A WELLS FARGO STAGECOACH, FOLLOWING THE USUAL ROUTE FROM DENVER TO SAN FRANCISCO, IS CARRYING A VERY LARGE CARGO OF GOLD. WELLS FARGO ALWAYS GETS THROUGH!"

I FOUND THIS WHEN I WAS CLEARING OUT THE WOODS...

IF ALL THE PAPERS WERE TOLD OF OUR TRIP BY TELEGRAPH, THE ATTACKS ARE GOING TO MULTIPLY!

THAT'S PART OF THE PLAN! ALL OF AMERICA HAS TO KNOW THAT WELLS FARGO ALWAYS GETS THROUGH!

WITH THIS KIND OF PROVOCATION, IT'LL END UP NEVER GETTING THROUGH AGAIN!

HEY! COULD I HAVE SOME OF MY GOLD?? MY LUCK HAS TURNED...

NOBODY'S TOUCHING THIS GOLD! AND I'D ADVISE YOU TO PLAY WITH CAT ONLY ON BUMPY GROUND!

10B

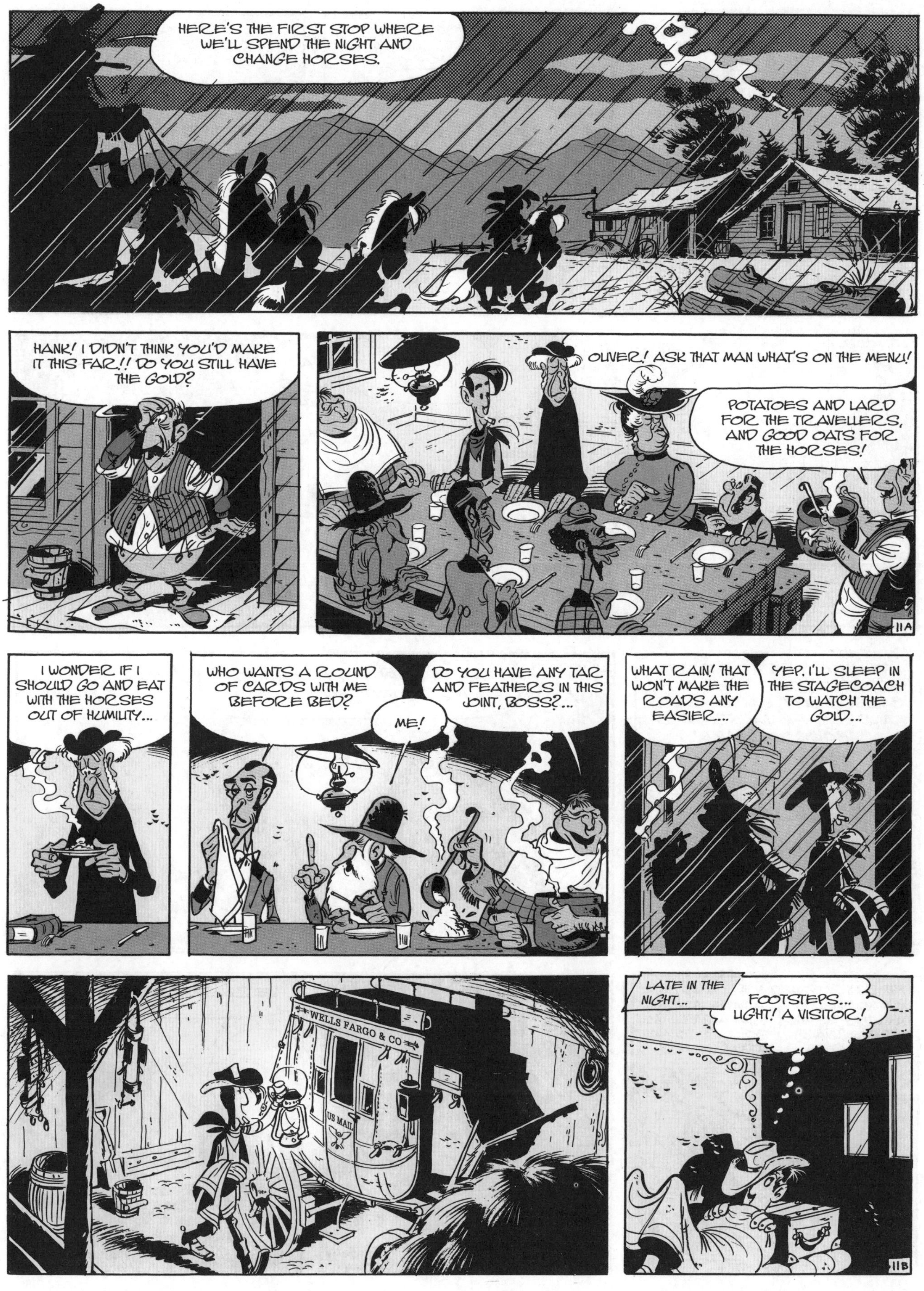
HERE'S THE FIRST STOP WHERE WE'LL SPEND THE NIGHT AND CHANGE HORSES.
HANK! I DIDN'T THINK YOU'D MAKE IT THIS FAR!! DO YOU STILL HAVE THE GOLD?
OLIVER! ASK THAT MAN WHAT'S ON THE MENU!
POTATOES AND LARD FOR THE TRAVELLERS, AND GOOD OATS FOR THE HORSES!
I WONDER IF I SHOULD GO AND EAT WITH THE HORSES OUT OF HUMILITY...
WHO WANTS A ROUND OF CARDS WITH ME BEFORE BED?
ME!
DO YOU HAVE ANY TAR AND FEATHERS IN THIS JOINT, BOSS?...
WHAT RAIN! THAT WON'T MAKE THE ROADS ANY EASIER...
YEP. I'LL SLEEP IN THE STAGECOACH TO WATCH THE GOLD...
WELLS FARGO & CO
US MAIL
LATE IN THE NIGHT...
FOOTSTEPS... LIGHT! A VISITOR!

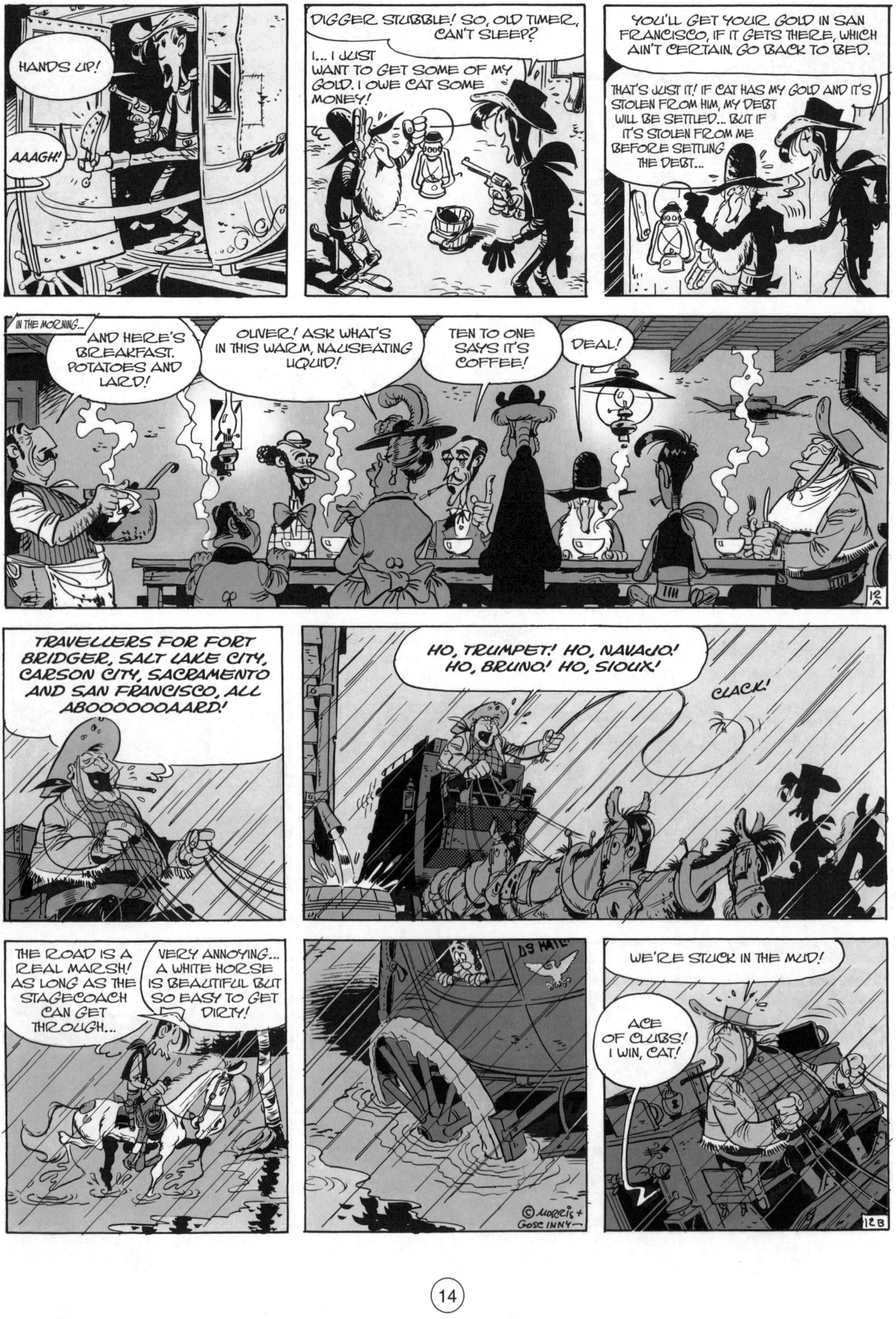
HANDS UP!
AAAGH!
DIGGER STUBBLE! SO, OLD TIMER, CAN'T SLEEP?
I... I JUST WANT TO GET SOME OF MY GOLD. I OWE CAT SOME MONEY!
YOU'LL GET YOUR GOLD IN SAN FRANCISCO, IF IT GETS THERE, WHICH AIN'T CERTAIN. GO BACK TO BED.
THAT'S JUST IT! IF CAT HAS MY GOLD AND IT'S STOLEN FROM HIM, MY DEBT WILL BE SETTLED... BUT IF IT'S STOLEN FROM ME BEFORE SETTLING THE DEBT...
IN THE MORNING...
AND HERE'S BREAKFAST. POTATOES AND LARD!
OLIVER! ASK WHAT'S IN THIS WARM, NAUSEATING LIQUID!
TEN TO ONE SAYS IT'S COFFEE!
DEAL!
12 A
TRAVELLERS FOR FORT BRIDGER, SALT LAKE CITY, CARSON CITY, SACRAMENTO AND SAN FRANCISCO, ALL ABOOOOOOOAARD!
HO, TRUMPET! HO, NAVAJO! HO, BRUNO! HO, SIOUX!
CLACK!
THE ROAD IS A REAL MARSH! AS LONG AS THE STAGECOACH CAN GET THROUGH...
VERY ANNOYING... A WHITE HORSE IS BEAUTIFUL BUT SO EASY TO GET DIRTY!
US MAIL
© MORRIS + GOSCINNY
WE'RE STUCK IN THE MUD!
ACE OF CLUBS! I WIN, CAT!
12 B

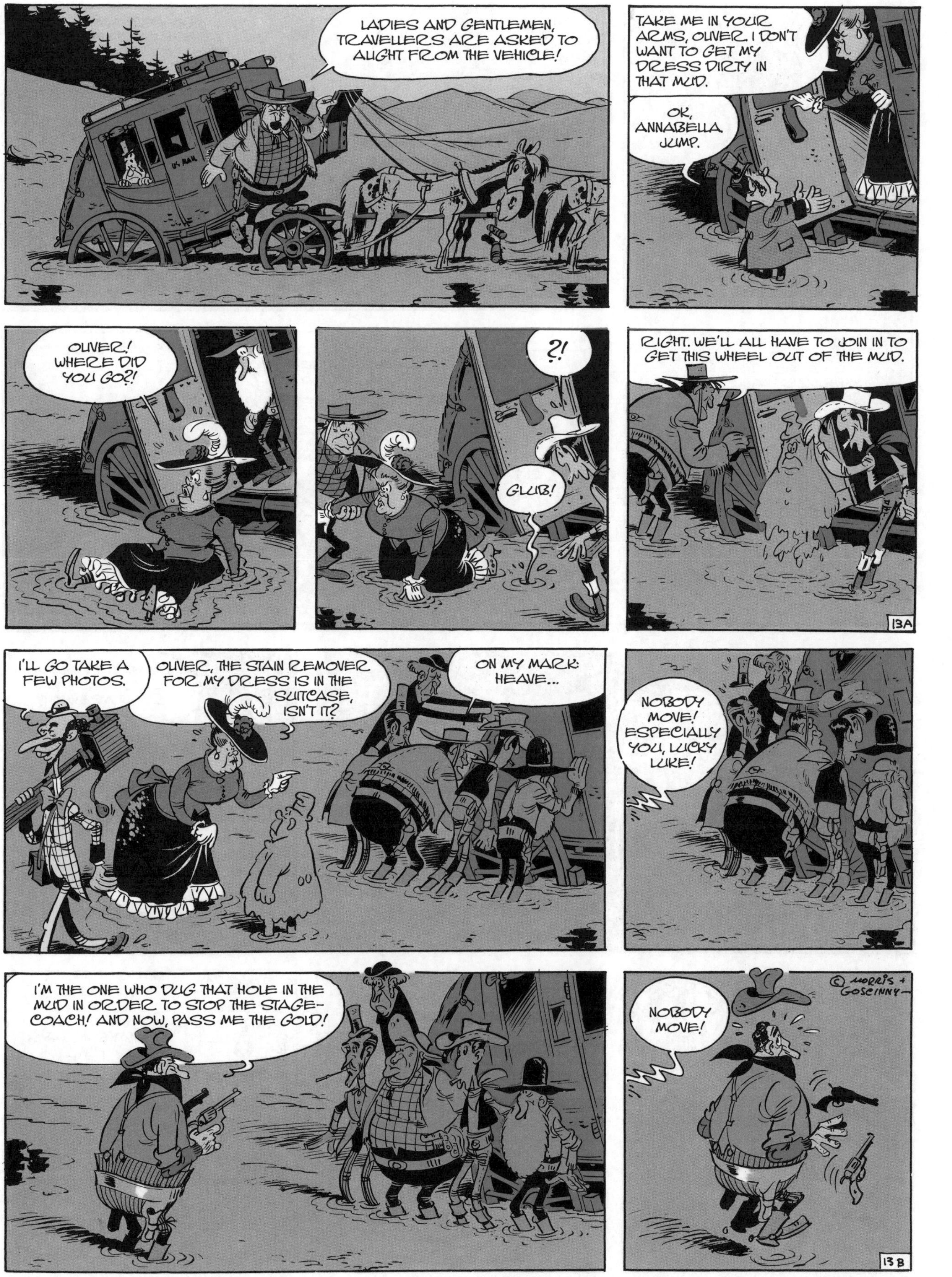
LADIES AND GENTLEMEN, TRAVELLERS ARE ASKED TO ALIGHT FROM THE VEHICLE!
TAKE ME IN YOUR ARMS, OLIVER. I DON'T WANT TO GET MY DRESS DIRTY IN THAT MUD.
OK, ANNABELLA. JUMP.
OLIVER! WHERE DID YOU GO?!
?!
GLUB!
RIGHT. WE'LL ALL HAVE TO JOIN IN TO GET THIS WHEEL OUT OF THE MUD.
13A
I'LL GO TAKE A FEW PHOTOS.
OLIVER, THE STAIN REMOVER FOR MY DRESS IS IN THE SUITCASE, ISN'T IT?
ON MY MARK: HEAVE...
NOBODY MOVE! ESPECIALLY YOU, LUCKY LUKE!
I'M THE ONE WHO DUG THAT HOLE IN THE MUD IN ORDER TO STOP THE STAGE-COACH! AND NOW, PASS ME THE GOLD!
© MORRIS + GOSCINNY
NOBODY MOVE!
13B

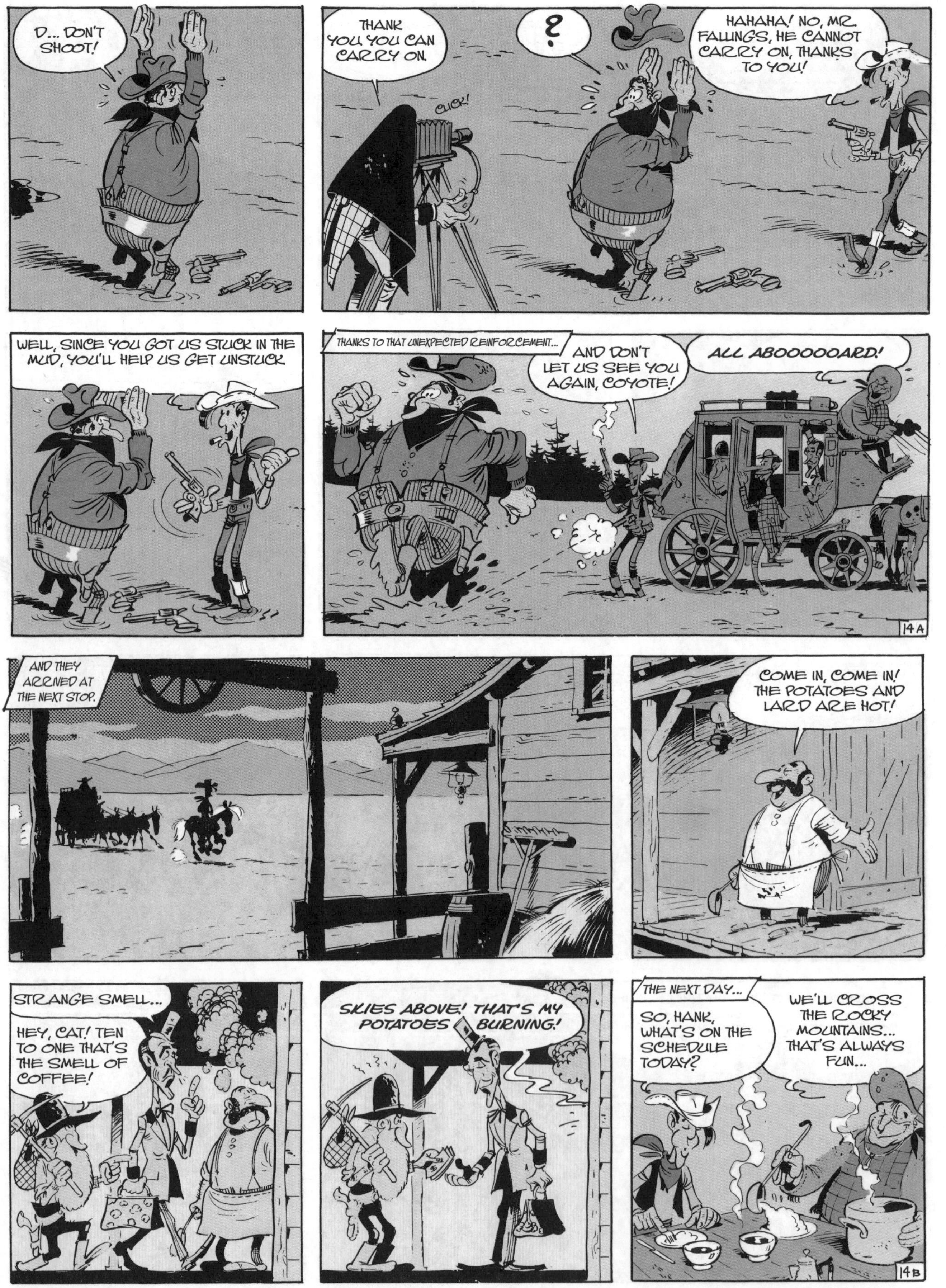
D... DON'T SHOOT!
THANK YOU YOU CAN CARRY ON.
CLICK!
?
HAHAHA! NO, MR FALLINGS, HE CANNOT CARRY ON, THANKS TO YOU!
WELL, SINCE YOU GOT US STUCK IN THE MUD, YOU'LL HELP US GET UNSTUCK
THANKS TO THAT UNEXPECTED REINFORCEMENT...
AND DON'T LET US SEE YOU AGAIN, COYOTE!
ALL ABOOOOOARD!
14 A
AND THEY ARRIVED AT THE NEXT STOP.
COME IN, COME IN! THE POTATOES AND LARD ARE HOT!
STRANGE SMELL...
HEY, CAT! TEN TO ONE THAT'S THE SMELL OF COFFEE!
SKIES ABOVE! THAT'S MY POTATOES BURNING!
THE NEXT DAY...
SO, HANK, WHAT'S ON THE SCHEDULE TODAY?
WE'LL CROSS THE ROCKY MOUNTAINS... THAT'S ALWAYS FUN...
14 B

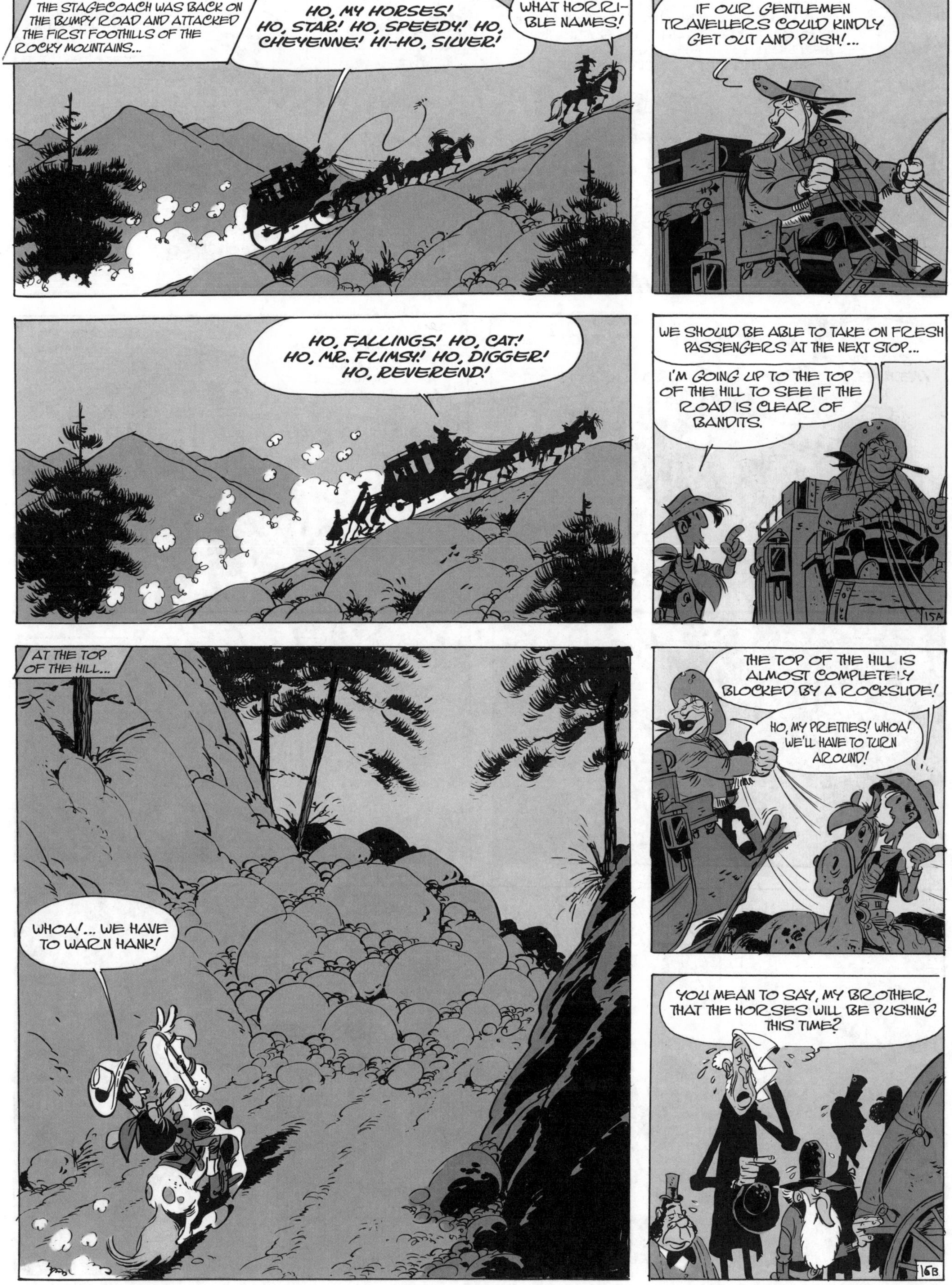
THE STAGECOACH WAS BACK ON THE BUMPY ROAD AND ATTACKED THE FIRST FOOTHILLS OF THE ROCKY MOUNTAINS...
HO, MY HORSES! HO, STAR! HO, SPEEDY! HO, CHEYENNE! HI-HO, SILVER!
WHAT HORRI-BLE NAMES!
IF OUR GENTLEMEN TRAVELLERS COULD KINDLY GET OUT AND PUSH!...
HO, FALLINGS! HO, CAT! HO, MR. FLIMSY! HO, DIGGER! HO, REVEREND!
WE SHOULD BE ABLE TO TAKE ON FRESH PASSENGERS AT THE NEXT STOP...
I'M GOING UP TO THE TOP OF THE HILL TO SEE IF THE ROAD IS CLEAR OF BANDITS.
AT THE TOP OF THE HILL...
WHOA!... WE HAVE TO WARN HANK!
THE TOP OF THE HILL IS ALMOST COMPLETELY BLOCKED BY A ROCKSLIDE!
HO, MY PRETTIES! WHOA! WE'LL HAVE TO TURN AROUND!
YOU MEAN TO SAY, MY BROTHER, THAT THE HORSES WILL BE PUSHING THIS TIME?

NO, I HAVE AN IDEA AT THE TOP OF THE HILL, WE'LL DETACH THE HORSES. THEY'LL GO THROUGH THE PASSAGE THAT'S STILL THERE. THEN WE'LL PUSH THE STAGECOACH OVER THE ROCKSLIDE USING OUR MEN...

... FINALLY, ON THE OTHER SIDE OF THE OBSTACLE, WE'LL REATTACH THE HORSES.

OH, REALLY? BECAUSE I WAS STARTING TO WONDER IF IT WAS EVEN WORTH BRINGING THEM ALONG...

ALL TOGETHER! HEAVE...

PUSH!

THAT'S IT, LUKE! THE HORSES ARE THROUGH.

IT'S GOING TO TIP OVER... HOLD IT TIGHT! THE DROP IS STRAIGHT DOWN BEHIND THE ROCKS! GENTLY!

GENTLY, OLIVER!

SNAP!

MY STAGE-COACH!

IT'S TEARING DOWN THE HILL!

MY CAMERA!

MY GOLD!

YOUR WIFE!

TEN TO ONE SHE MAKES IT!

DEAL!

© MORRIS + GOSCINNY

16

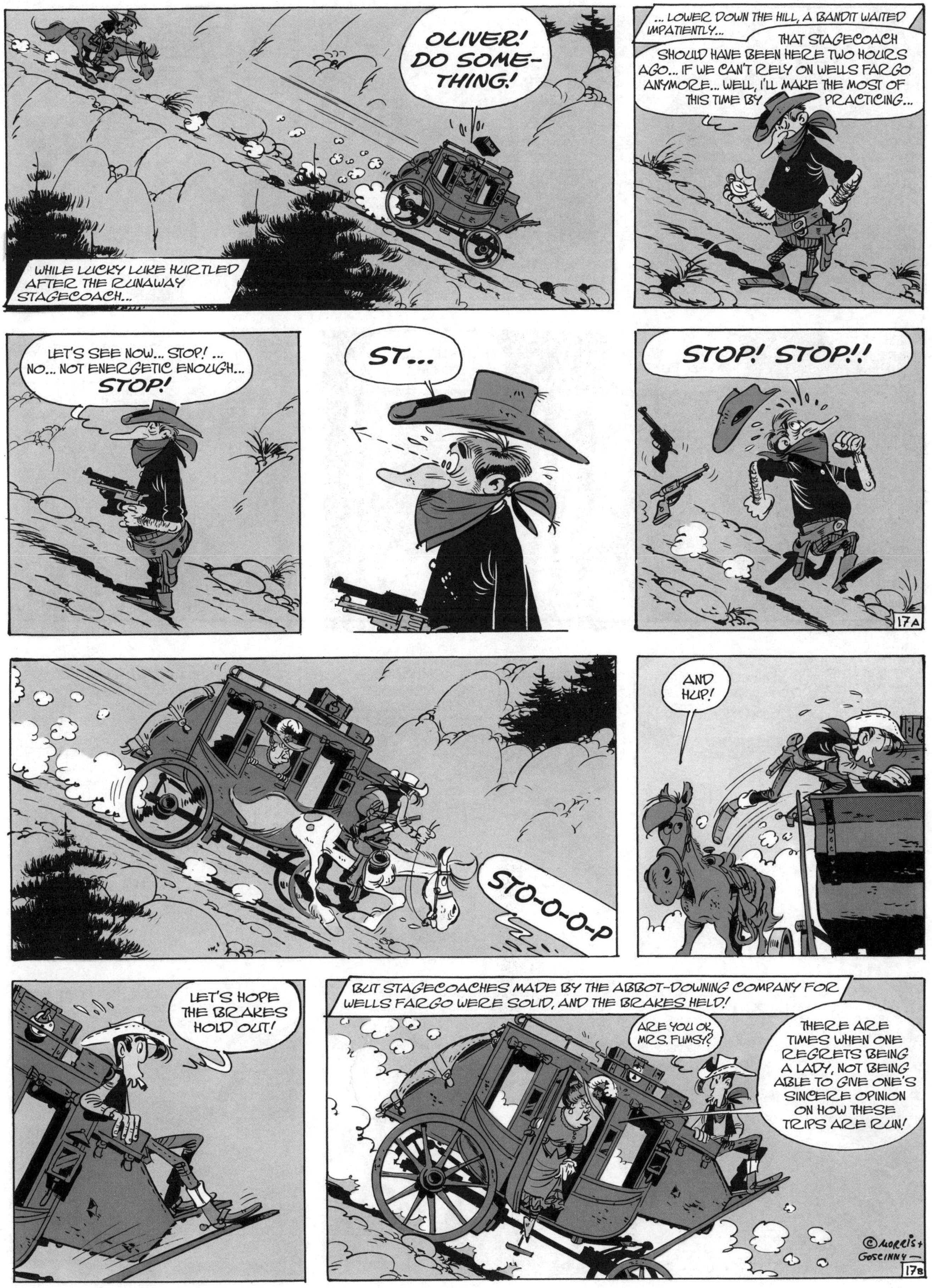
OLIVER! DO SOME-THING!
WHILE LUCKY LUKE HURTLED AFTER THE RUNAWAY STAGECOACH...
... LOWER DOWN THE HILL, A BANDIT WAITED IMPATIENTLY...
THAT STAGECOACH SHOULD HAVE BEEN HERE TWO HOURS AGO... IF WE CAN'T RELY ON WELLS FARGO ANYMORE... WELL, I'LL MAKE THE MOST OF THIS TIME BY PRACTICING...
LET'S SEE NOW... STOP! ... NO... NOT ENERGETIC ENOUGH... STOP!
ST...
STOP! STOP!!
17A
STO-O-O-P
AND HUP!
LET'S HOPE THE BRAKES HOLD OUT!
BUT STAGECOACHES MADE BY THE ABBOT-DOWNING COMPANY FOR WELLS FARGO WERE SOLID, AND THE BRAKES HELD!
ARE YOU OK, MRS. FUMSY?
THERE ARE TIMES WHEN ONE REGRETS BEING A LADY, NOT BEING ABLE TO GIVE ONE'S SINCERE OPINION ON HOW THESE TRIPS ARE RUN!
© MORRIS + GOSCINNY
17B

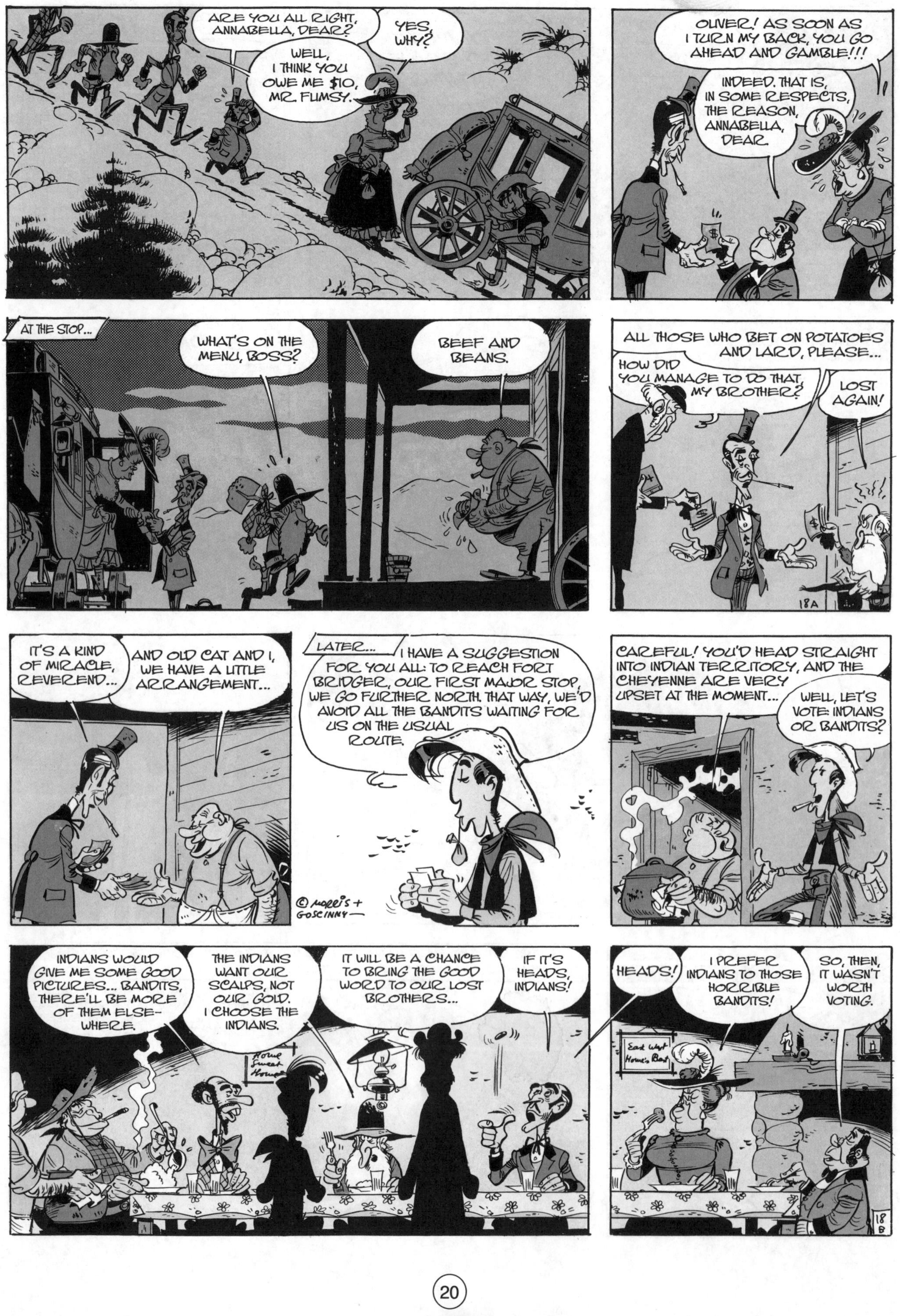
ARE YOU ALL RIGHT, ANNABELLA, DEAR?
YES, WHY?
WELL, I THINK YOU OWE ME $10, MR. FUMSY.
OLIVER! AS SOON AS I TURN MY BACK, YOU GO AHEAD AND GAMBLE!!!
INDEED. THAT IS, IN SOME RESPECTS, THE REASON, ANNABELLA, DEAR.
AT THE STOP...
WHAT'S ON THE MENU, BOSS?
BEEF AND BEANS.
ALL THOSE WHO BET ON POTATOES AND LARD, PLEASE...
HOW DID YOU MANAGE TO DO THAT, MY BROTHER?
LOST AGAIN!
18A
IT'S A KIND OF MIRACLE, REVEREND...
AND OLD CAT AND I, WE HAVE A LITTLE ARRANGEMENT...
LATER...
I HAVE A SUGGESTION FOR YOU ALL: TO REACH FORT BRIDGER, OUR FIRST MAJOR STOP, WE GO FURTHER NORTH. THAT WAY, WE'D AVOID ALL THE BANDITS WAITING FOR US ON THE USUAL ROUTE.
© MORRIS + GOSCINNY
CAREFUL! YOU'D HEAD STRAIGHT INTO INDIAN TERRITORY, AND THE CHEYENNE ARE VERY UPSET AT THE MOMENT...
WELL, LET'S VOTE: INDIANS OR BANDITS?
INDIANS WOULD GIVE ME SOME GOOD PICTURES... BANDITS, THERE'LL BE MORE OF THEM ELSE-WHERE.
THE INDIANS WANT OUR SCALPS, NOT OUR GOLD. I CHOOSE THE INDIANS.
IT WILL BE A CHANCE TO BRING THE GOOD WORD TO OUR LOST BROTHERS...
IF IT'S HEADS, INDIANS!
Home Sweet Home
HEADS!
I PREFER INDIANS TO THOSE HORRIBLE BANDITS!
SO, THEN, IT WASN'T WORTH VOTING.
East West Home's Best
18B

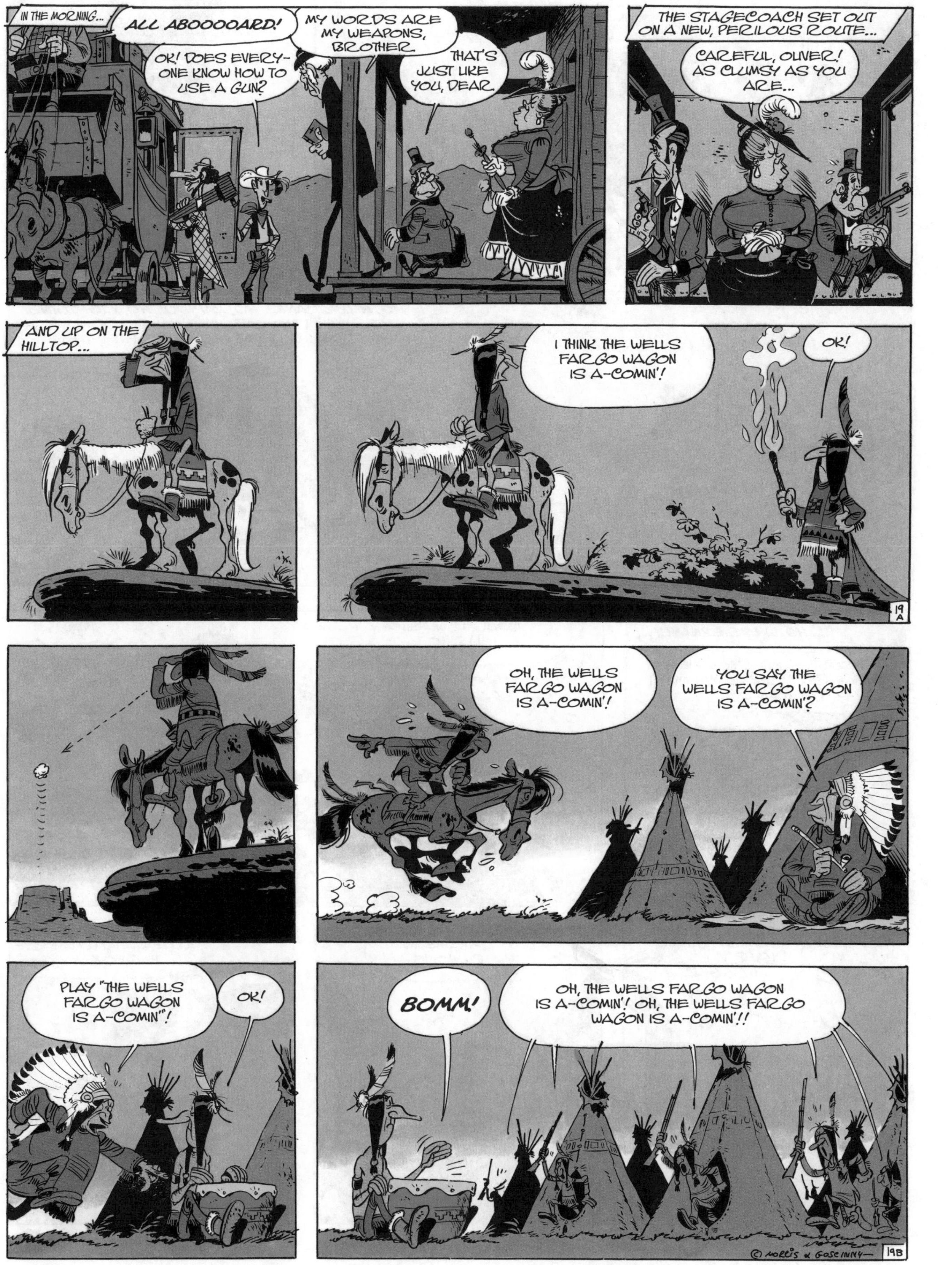

IN THE MORNING...
ALL ABOOOOARD!
OK! DOES EVERYONE KNOW HOW TO USE A GUN?
MY WORDS ARE MY WEAPONS, BROTHER
THAT'S JUST LIKE YOU, DEAR
THE STAGECOACH SET OUT ON A NEW, PERILOUS ROUTE...
CAREFUL, OLIVER! AS CLUMSY AS YOU ARE...
AND UP ON THE HILLTOP...
I THINK THE WELLS FARGO WAGON IS A-COMIN'!
OK!
19 A
OH, THE WELLS FARGO WAGON IS A-COMIN'!
YOU SAY THE WELLS FARGO WAGON IS A-COMIN'?
PLAY "THE WELLS FARGO WAGON IS A-COMIN'"!
OK!
BOMM!
OH, THE WELLS FARGO WAGON IS A-COMIN'! OH, THE WELLS FARGO WAGON IS A-COMIN'!!
© MORRIS & GOSCINNY
19B

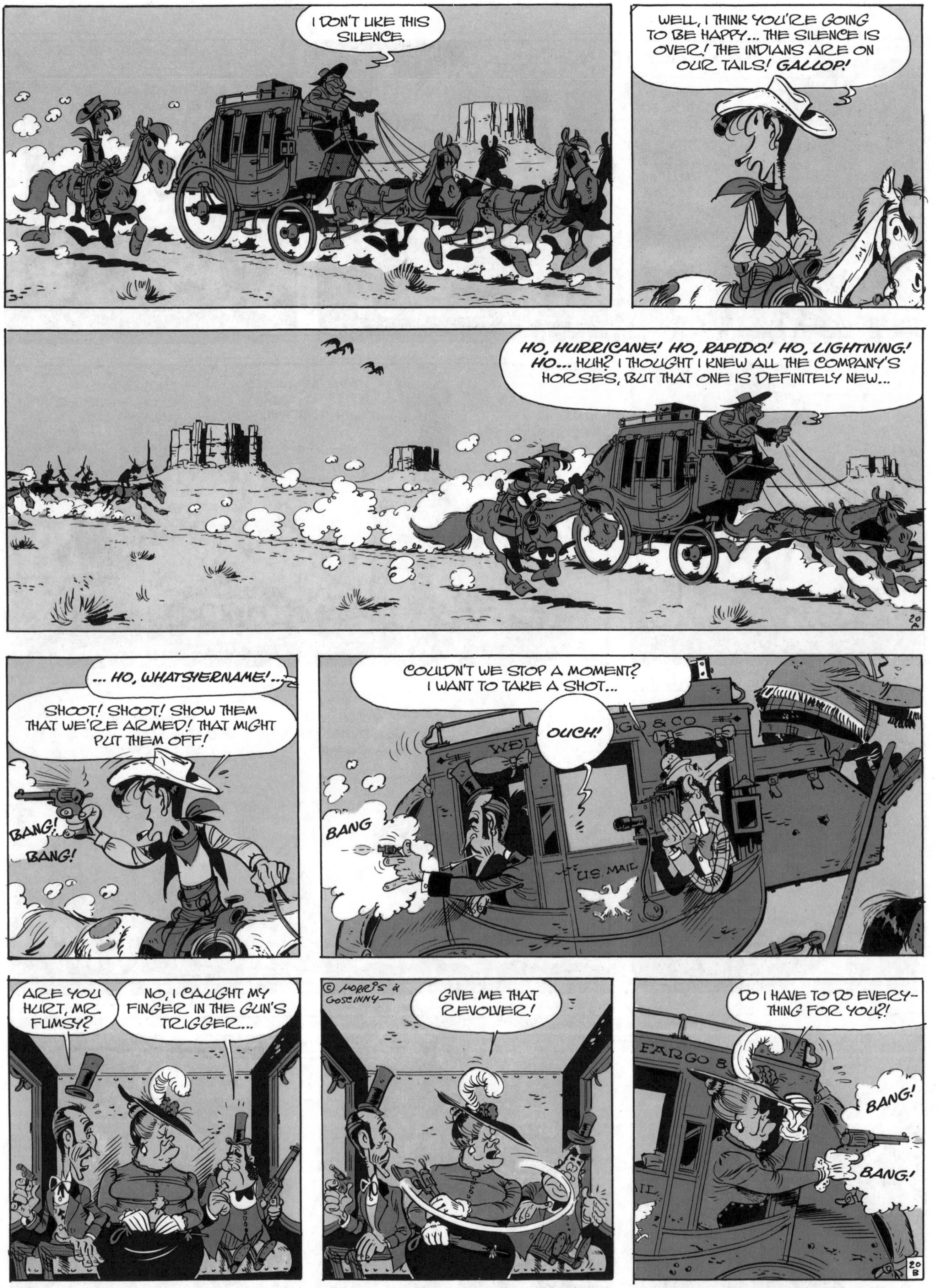
I DON'T LIKE THIS SILENCE.
WELL, I THINK YOU'RE GOING TO BE HAPPY... THE SILENCE IS OVER! THE INDIANS ARE ON OUR TAILS! GALLOP!
HO, HURRICANE! HO, RAPIDO! HO, LIGHTNING! HO... HUH? I THOUGHT I KNEW ALL THE COMPANY'S HORSES, BUT THAT ONE IS DEFINITELY NEW...
... HO, WHATSYERNAME! ...
SHOOT! SHOOT! SHOW THEM THAT WE'RE ARMED! THAT MIGHT PUT THEM OFF!
BANG!
BANG!
COULDN'T WE STOP A MOMENT? I WANT TO TAKE A SHOT...
OUCH!
BANG
U.S. MAIL
ARE YOU HURT, MR. FUMSY?
NO, I CAUGHT MY FINGER IN THE GUN'S TRIGGER...
© MORRIS & GOSCINNY
GIVE ME THAT REVOLVER!
DO I HAVE TO DO EVERYTHING FOR YOU?!
BANG!
BANG!

THEY'RE NOT BEING PUT OFF, BUT THEY'RE STAYING OUT OF OUR GUNS' RANGE. THEY HAVE A PLAN.
THERE'S THEIR PLAN! STRAIGHT AHEAD!
WE'RE SURROUND-ED... AND THEY HAVE RIFLES!
YEP, THE GOOD OLD DAYS WHERE WE HAD THE GUNS AND THEY HAD THE ARROWS ARE GONE... IT MAKES DIALOGUE DIFFICULT...
21A
DRIVER! WHY ARE WE STOPPING?
THERE ARE TOO MANY OF THEM AND THEY'RE TOO STRONG, MRS. FUMSY. WE MUST PARLEY.
YOU SHOULD GIVE ALL YOUR GLASS JEWELLERY FOR THE PARLEY, DEAR.
MY JEWELLERY?! MY FAMILY JEWELS?! ARE YOU CRAZY, OLIVER!
TRY TO RUN IF I CAN'T CONVINCE THEM, HANK...
OK! NICE TO HAVE MET YOU, LUCKY...
HOW! I SALUTE MY NATIVE BROTHERS. CAN ONE OF YOU SPEAK MY LANGUAGE?
YES!
TELL YOUR CHIEF THAT THE PALEFACES ARE ONLY PASSING THROUGH HIS HUNTING GROUNDS. THEY ASK HIM FOR PERMISSION TO CONTINUE THEIR JOURNEY.
© MORRIS + GOSCINNY
21B

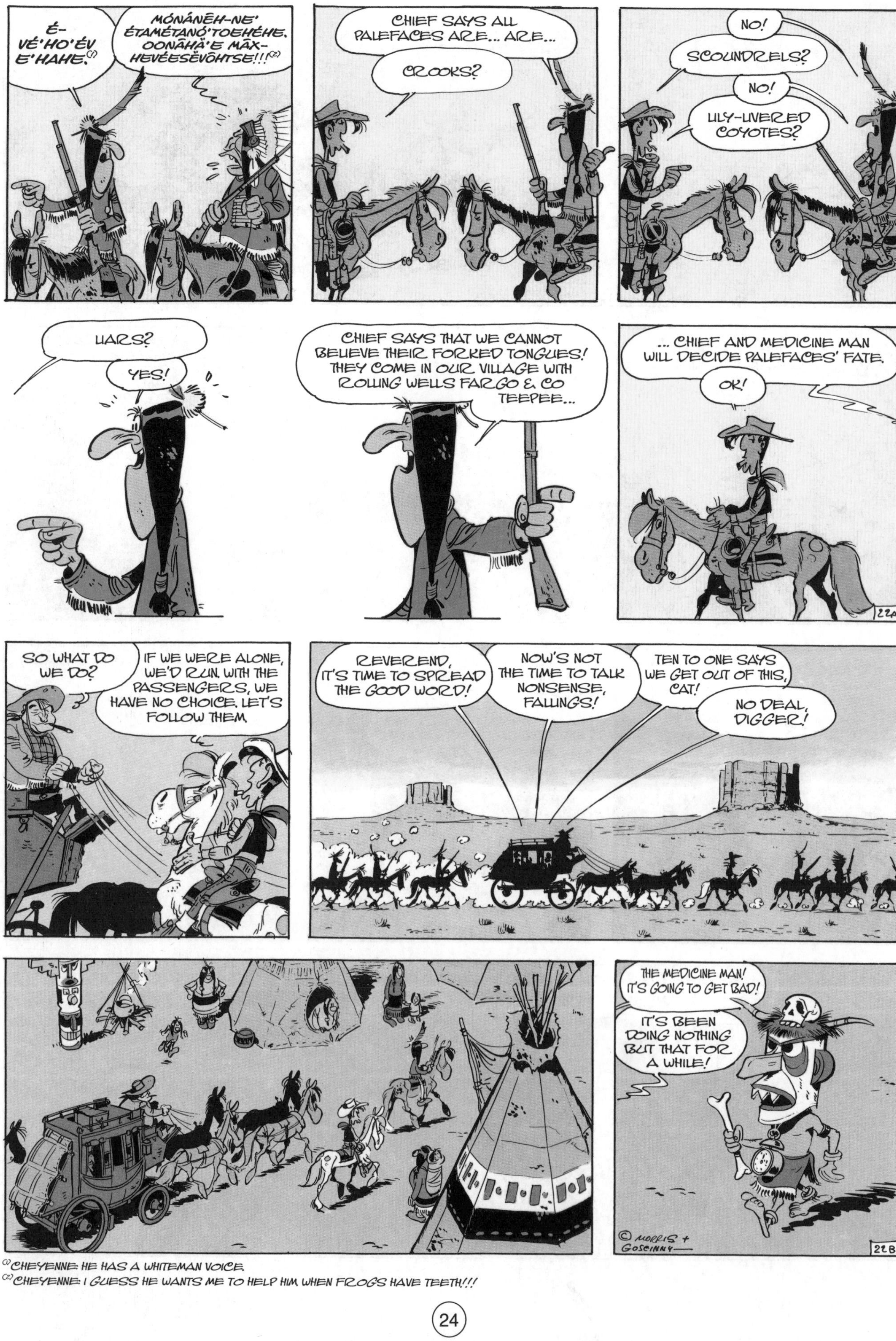
É-VÉ'HO'ÉV E'HAHE.(1)
MÓNÁNÊH-NE' ÉTAMÉTANÓ'TOEHÉHE. OONÃHÄ'E MÃX-HEVÉESËVÕHTSE!!!(2)
CHIEF SAYS ALL PALEFACES ARE... ARE...
CROOKS?
NO!
SCOUNDRELS?
NO!
LILY-LIVERED COYOTES?
LIARS?
YES!
CHIEF SAYS THAT WE CANNOT BELIEVE THEIR FORKED TONGUES! THEY COME IN OUR VILLAGE WITH ROLLING WELLS FARGO & CO TEEPEE...
... CHIEF AND MEDICINE MAN WILL DECIDE PALEFACES' FATE.
OK!
22A
SO WHAT DO WE DO?
IF WE WERE ALONE, WE'D RUN. WITH THE PASSENGERS, WE HAVE NO CHOICE. LET'S FOLLOW THEM.
REVEREND, IT'S TIME TO SPREAD THE GOOD WORD!
NOW'S NOT THE TIME TO TALK NONSENSE, FALLINGS!
TEN TO ONE SAYS WE GET OUT OF THIS, CAT!
NO DEAL, DIGGER!
THE MEDICINE MAN! IT'S GOING TO GET BAD!
IT'S BEEN DOING NOTHING BUT THAT FOR A WHILE!
© MORRIS + GOSCINNY
22B

(1) CHEYENNE: HE HAS A WHITEMAN VOICE.

(2) CHEYENNE: I GUESS HE WANTS ME TO HELP HIM WHEN FROGS HAVE TEETH!!!

THAT MAN MUST BE RESPONSIBLE FOR THIS DELAY. I'LL SORT IT ALL OUT.

MRS. FUMSY, NO!

SIR, WE'VE HAD A TIRING JOURNEY, AND THESE INCIDENTS ARE HOLDING US UP EVEN MORE. MY HUSBAND, MR. FUMSY, IS EXPECTED IN SAN FRANCISCO TO START HIS NEW JOB AS AN ACCOUNTANT...

ALSO, TO BUY OUR FREEDOM AND THAT OF OUR COMPANIONS, I OFFER YOU ONE OF THESE JEWELS THAT WERE MY MOTHER'S. CHOOSE ONE.

É-ÉŠKÓSE'HAHE![1]

MEDICINE MAN SAYS: FAKE.

VULGAR CHARACTER!

É-HEO' KEMÉÁ'HA![2]

MEDICINE MAN SAYS HIM HAVE SEEN IN THE SIGNS THAT WE MUST KILL PALEFACES.

OLIVER! STOP SMILING!

ASK THE MEDICINE MAN IF HE KNOWS HOW TO PLAY POKER. IF HE KNOWS, WE COULD...

LET ME TALK, CAT

TELL THE GREAT CHIEF THAT HIS MEDICINE MAN IS TALKING LIKE A BABBLING PAPOOSE...

WE HAVE WITH US A GREAT MEDICINE MAN, AND IF WE AREN'T LEFT IN PEACE, HE'LL BRING GREAT MISFORTUNE ON THE SCALPS OF OUR NATIVE BROTHERS!

HOHOHO!

MEDICINE MAN LAUGH.

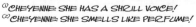

[1] CHEYENNE: SHE HAS A SHRILL VOICE!
[2] CHEYENNE: SHE SMELLS LIKE PERFUME!

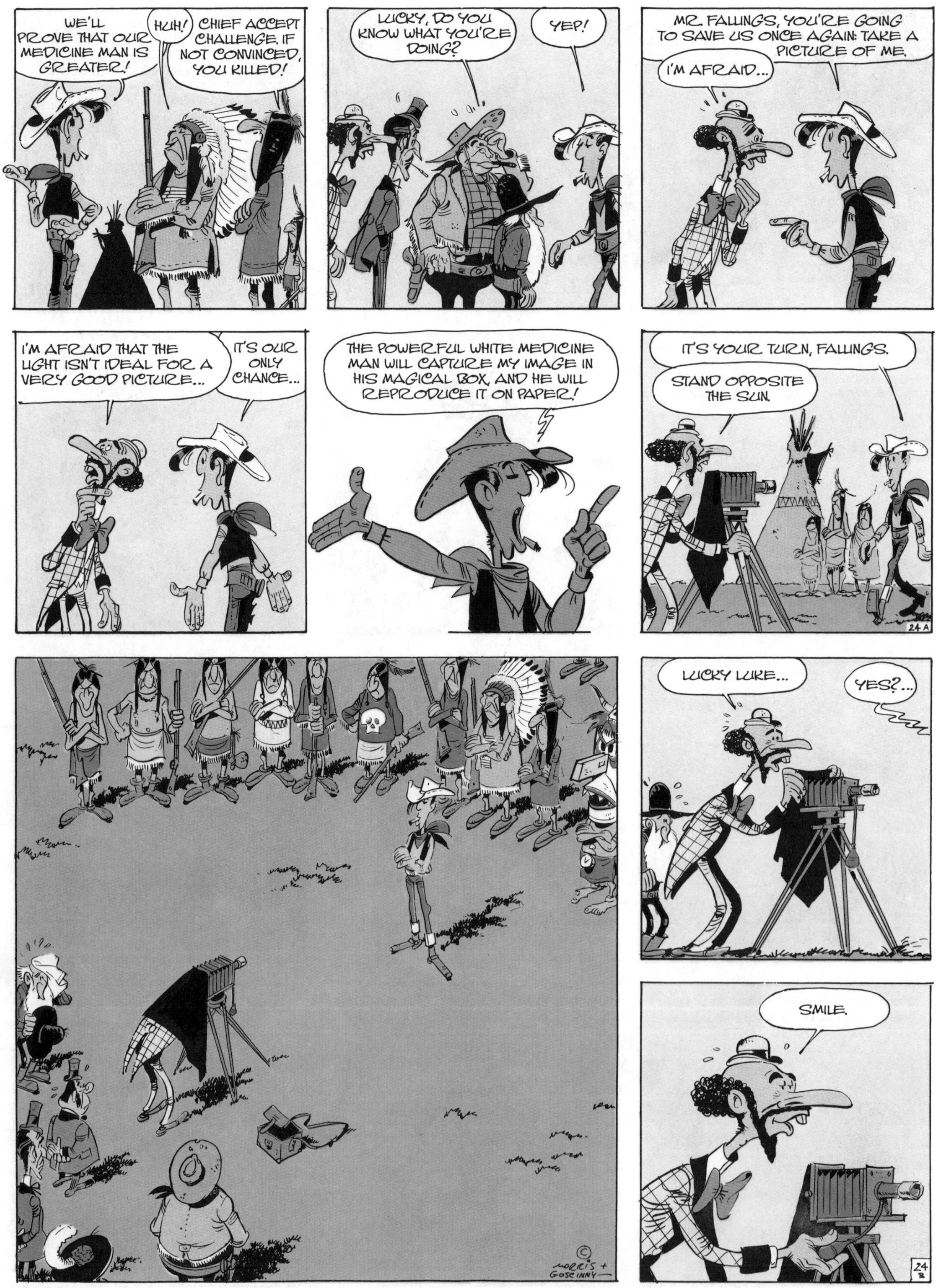
WE'LL PROVE THAT OUR MEDICINE MAN IS GREATER!
HUH!
CHIEF ACCEPT CHALLENGE. IF NOT CONVINCED, YOU KILLED!
LUCKY, DO YOU KNOW WHAT YOU'RE DOING?
YEP!
MR. FALLINGS, YOU'RE GOING TO SAVE US ONCE AGAIN: TAKE A PICTURE OF ME.
I'M AFRAID...
I'M AFRAID THAT THE LIGHT ISN'T IDEAL FOR A VERY GOOD PICTURE...
IT'S OUR ONLY CHANCE...
THE POWERFUL WHITE MEDICINE MAN WILL CAPTURE MY IMAGE IN HIS MAGICAL BOX, AND HE WILL REPRODUCE IT ON PAPER!
IT'S YOUR TURN, FALLINGS.
STAND OPPOSITE THE SUN.
24 A
MORRIS + GOSCINNY
LUCKY LUKE...
YES?...
SMILE.
24 B

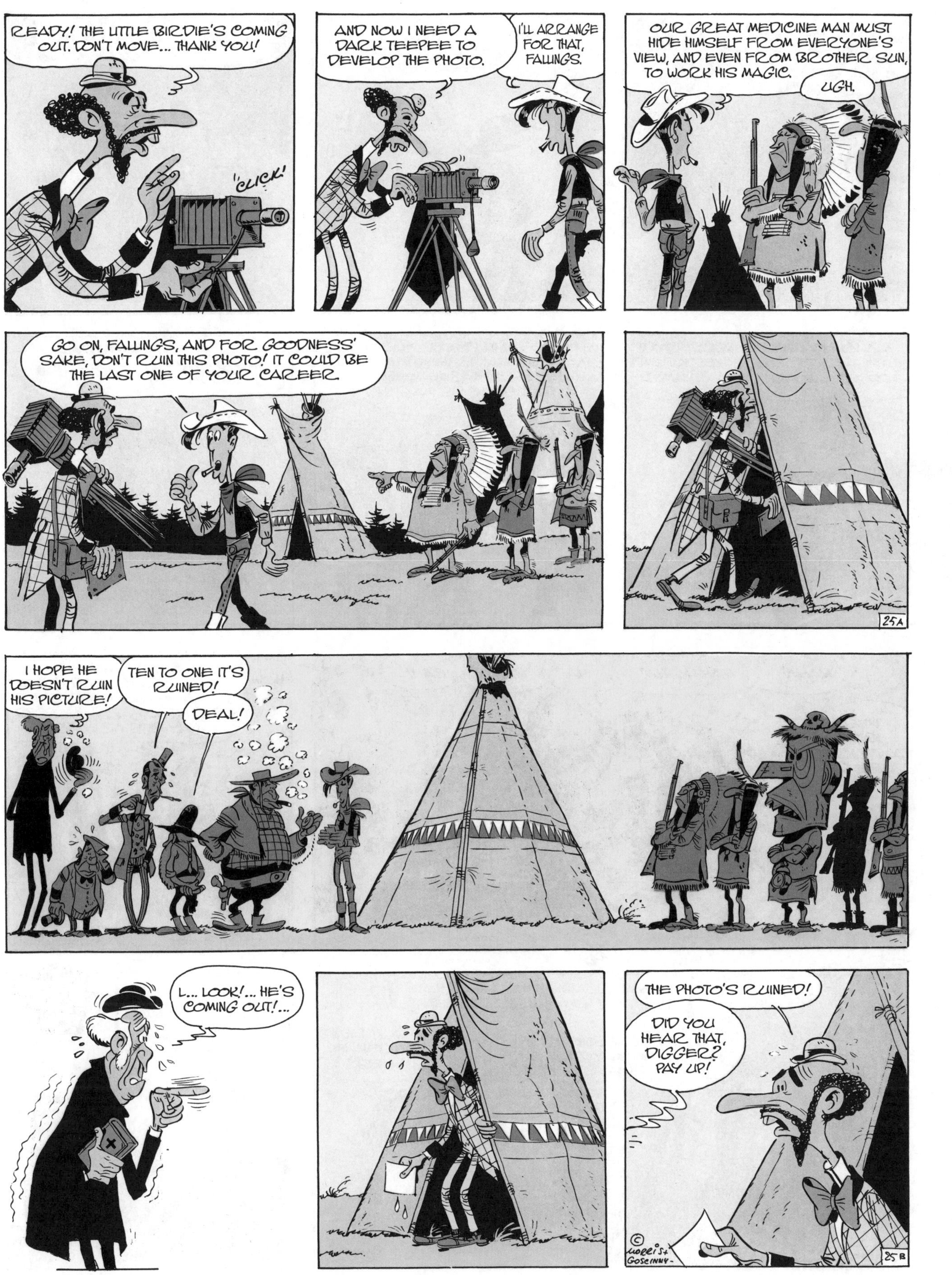
READY! THE LITTLE BIRDIE'S COMING OUT. DON'T MOVE... THANK YOU!
CLICK!
AND NOW I NEED A DARK TEEPEE TO DEVELOP THE PHOTO.
I'LL ARRANGE FOR THAT, FALLINGS.
OUR GREAT MEDICINE MAN MUST HIDE HIMSELF FROM EVERYONE'S VIEW, AND EVEN FROM BROTHER SUN, TO WORK HIS MAGIC.
UGH.
GO ON, FALLINGS, AND FOR GOODNESS' SAKE, DON'T RUIN THIS PHOTO! IT COULD BE THE LAST ONE OF YOUR CAREER.
25A
I HOPE HE DOESN'T RUIN HIS PICTURE!
TEN TO ONE IT'S RUINED!
DEAL!
L... LOOK!... HE'S COMING OUT!...
THE PHOTO'S RUINED!
DID YOU HEAR THAT, DIGGER? PAY UP!
© MORRIS + GOSCINNY
25B

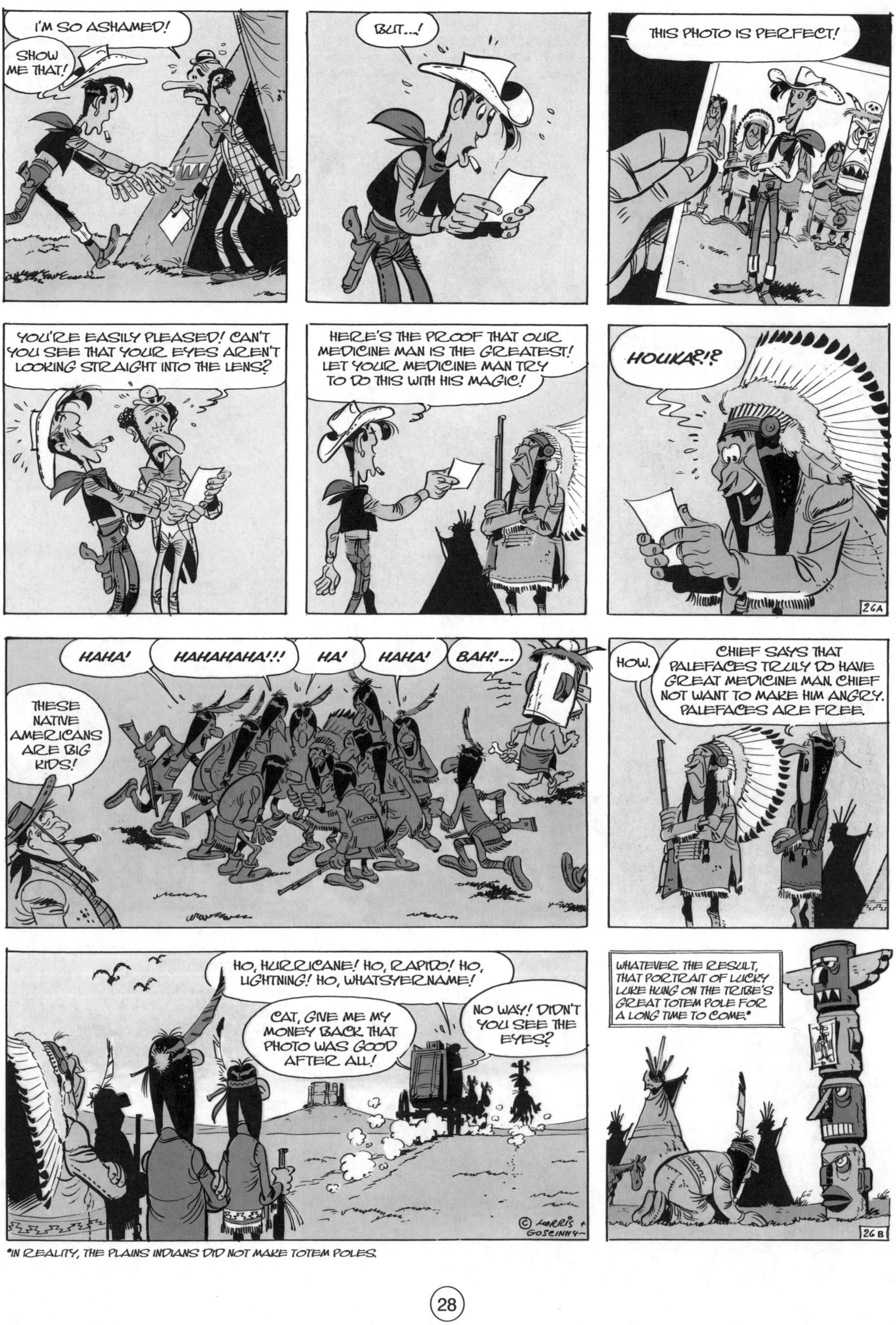
I'M SO ASHAMED!
SHOW ME THAT!
BUT...!
THIS PHOTO IS PERFECT!
YOU'RE EASILY PLEASED! CAN'T YOU SEE THAT YOUR EYES AREN'T LOOKING STRAIGHT INTO THE LENS?
HERE'S THE PROOF THAT OUR MEDICINE MAN IS THE GREATEST! LET YOUR MEDICINE MAN TRY TO DO THIS WITH HIS MAGIC!
HOUKA?!?
26A
HAHA!
HAHAHAHA!!!
HA!
HAHA!
BAH!...
THESE NATIVE AMERICANS ARE BIG KIDS!
HOW.
CHIEF SAYS THAT PALEFACES TRULY DO HAVE GREAT MEDICINE MAN. CHIEF NOT WANT TO MAKE HIM ANGRY. PALEFACES ARE FREE.
HO, HURRICANE! HO, RAPIDO! HO, LIGHTNING! HO, WHATSYERNAME!
CAT, GIVE ME MY MONEY BACK THAT PHOTO WAS GOOD AFTER ALL!
NO WAY! DIDN'T YOU SEE THE EYES?
© MORRIS + GOSCINNY
WHATEVER THE RESULT, THAT PORTRAIT OF LUCKY LUKE HUNG ON THE TRIBE'S GREAT TOTEM POLE FOR A LONG TIME TO COME.*
26B

*IN REALITY, THE PLAINS INDIANS DID NOT MAKE TOTEM POLES.

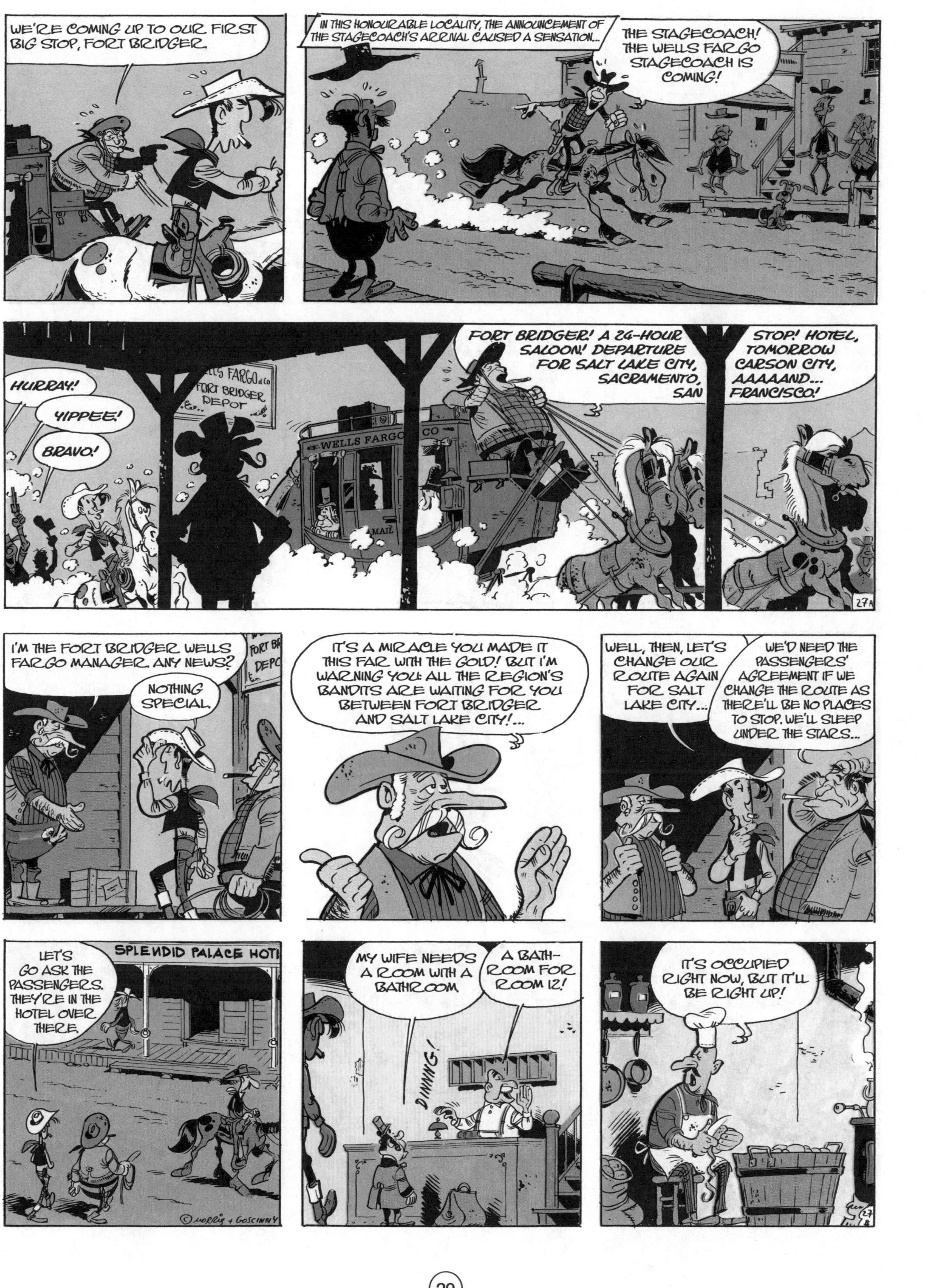
WE'RE COMING UP TO OUR FIRST BIG STOP, FORT BRIDGER.
IN THIS HONOURABLE LOCALITY, THE ANNOUNCEMENT OF THE STAGECOACH'S ARRIVAL CAUSED A SENSATION...
THE STAGECOACH! THE WELLS FARGO STAGECOACH IS COMING!
HURRAY!
YIPPEE!
BRAVO!
WELLS FARGO & CO FORT BRIDGER DEPOT
WELLS FARGO & CO
MAIL
FORT BRIDGER! A 24-HOUR SALOON! DEPARTURE FOR SALT LAKE CITY, SACRAMENTO, SAN
STOP! HOTEL, TOMORROW CARSON CITY, AAAAAND... FRANCISCO!
I'M THE FORT BRIDGER WELLS FARGO MANAGER. ANY NEWS?
NOTHING SPECIAL.
IT'S A MIRACLE YOU MADE IT THIS FAR WITH THE GOLD! BUT I'M WARNING YOU: ALL THE REGION'S BANDITS ARE WAITING FOR YOU BETWEEN FORT BRIDGER AND SALT LAKE CITY!...
WELL, THEN, LET'S CHANGE OUR ROUTE AGAIN FOR SALT LAKE CITY...
WE'D NEED THE PASSENGERS' AGREEMENT IF WE CHANGE THE ROUTE AS THERE'LL BE NO PLACES TO STOP. WE'LL SLEEP UNDER THE STARS...
SPLENDID PALACE HOT
LET'S GO ASK THE PASSENGERS. THEY'RE IN THE HOTEL OVER THERE.
© MORRIS + GOSCINNY
MY WIFE NEEDS A ROOM WITH A BATHROOM.
A BATH-ROOM FOR ROOM 12!
DINNNG!
IT'S OCCUPIED RIGHT NOW, BUT IT'LL BE RIGHT UP!

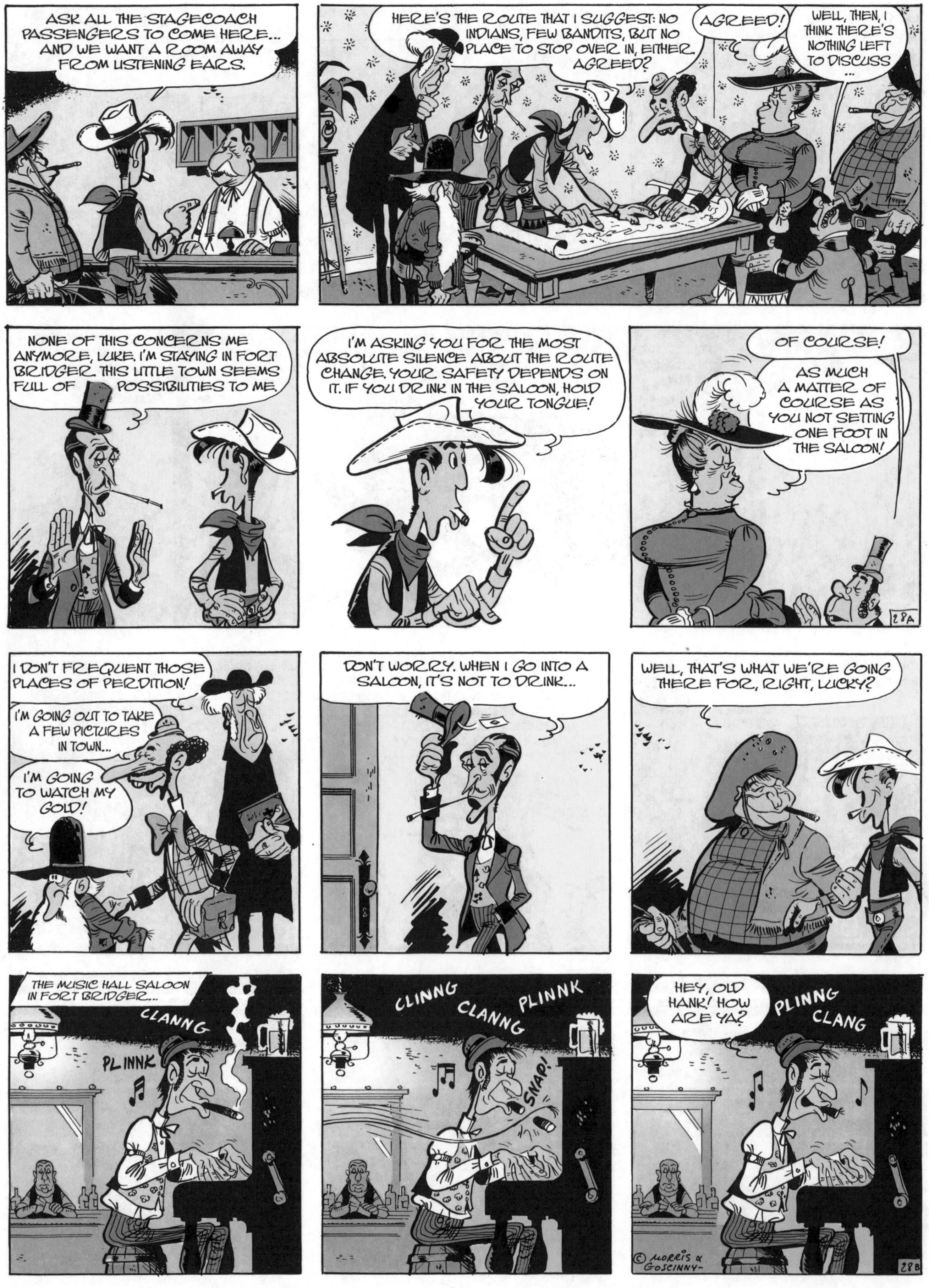
ASK ALL THE STAGECOACH PASSENGERS TO COME HERE... AND WE WANT A ROOM AWAY FROM LISTENING EARS.
HERE'S THE ROUTE THAT I SUGGEST: NO INDIANS, FEW BANDITS, BUT NO PLACE TO STOP OVER IN, EITHER. AGREED?
AGREED!
WELL, THEN, I THINK THERE'S NOTHING LEFT TO DISCUSS...
NONE OF THIS CONCERNS ME ANYMORE, LUKE. I'M STAYING IN FORT BRIDGER. THIS LITTLE TOWN SEEMS FULL OF POSSIBILITIES TO ME.
I'M ASKING YOU FOR THE MOST ABSOLUTE SILENCE ABOUT THE ROUTE CHANGE. YOUR SAFETY DEPENDS ON IT. IF YOU DRINK IN THE SALOON, HOLD YOUR TONGUE!
OF COURSE!
AS MUCH A MATTER OF COURSE AS YOU NOT SETTING ONE FOOT IN THE SALOON!
28A
I DON'T FREQUENT THOSE PLACES OF PERDITION!
I'M GOING OUT TO TAKE A FEW PICTURES IN TOWN...
I'M GOING TO WATCH MY GOLD!
DON'T WORRY. WHEN I GO INTO A SALOON, IT'S NOT TO DRINK...
WELL, THAT'S WHAT WE'RE GOING THERE FOR, RIGHT, LUCKY?
THE MUSIC HALL SALOON IN FORT BRIDGER...
CLANNG
PLINNK
CLINNG
CLANNG
PLINNK
SNAP!
HEY, OLD HANK! HOW ARE YA?
PLINNG
CLANG
© MORRIS & GOSCINNY
28B

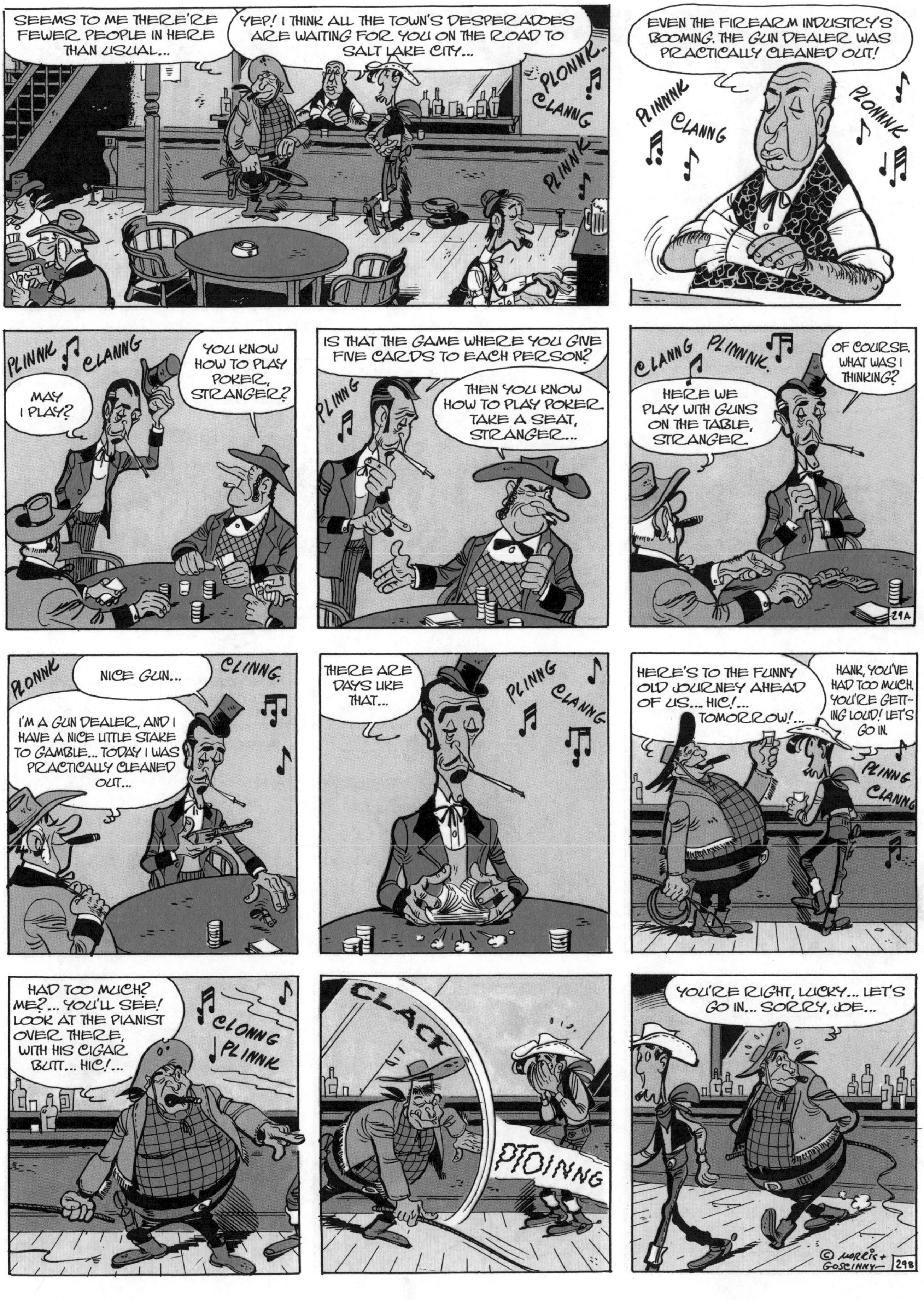
SEEMS TO ME THERE'RE FEWER PEOPLE IN HERE THAN USUAL...
YEP! I THINK ALL THE TOWN'S DESPERADOES ARE WAITING FOR YOU ON THE ROAD TO SALT LAKE CITY...
PLONNK
CLANNG
PLINNK
EVEN THE FIREARM INDUSTRY'S BOOMING. THE GUN DEALER WAS PRACTICALLY CLEANED OUT!
PLINNNK
CLANNG
PLONNNK
PLINNK
CLANNG
YOU KNOW HOW TO PLAY POKER, STRANGER?
MAY I PLAY?
IS THAT THE GAME WHERE YOU GIVE FIVE CARDS TO EACH PERSON?
PLINNG
THEN YOU KNOW HOW TO PLAY POKER. TAKE A SEAT, STRANGER...
CLANNG
PLINNNK.
HERE WE PLAY WITH GUNS ON THE TABLE, STRANGER.
OF COURSE. WHAT WAS I THINKING?
29A
PLONNK
NICE GUN...
CLINNG.
I'M A GUN DEALER, AND I HAVE A NICE LITTLE STAKE TO GAMBLE... TODAY I WAS PRACTICALLY CLEANED OUT...
THERE ARE DAYS LIKE THAT...
PLINNG
CLANNG
HERE'S TO THE FUNNY OLD JOURNEY AHEAD OF US... HIC!... TOMORROW!...
HANK, YOU'VE HAD TOO MUCH. YOU'RE GETTING LOUD! LET'S GO IN.
PLINNG
CLANING
HAD TOO MUCH? ME?... YOU'LL SEE! LOOK AT THE PIANIST OVER THERE, WITH HIS CIGAR BUTT... HIC!...
CLONNG
PLINNK
CLACK
PTOINNG
YOU'RE RIGHT, LUCKY... LET'S GO IN... SORRY, JOE...
© MORRIS + GOSCINNY
29B

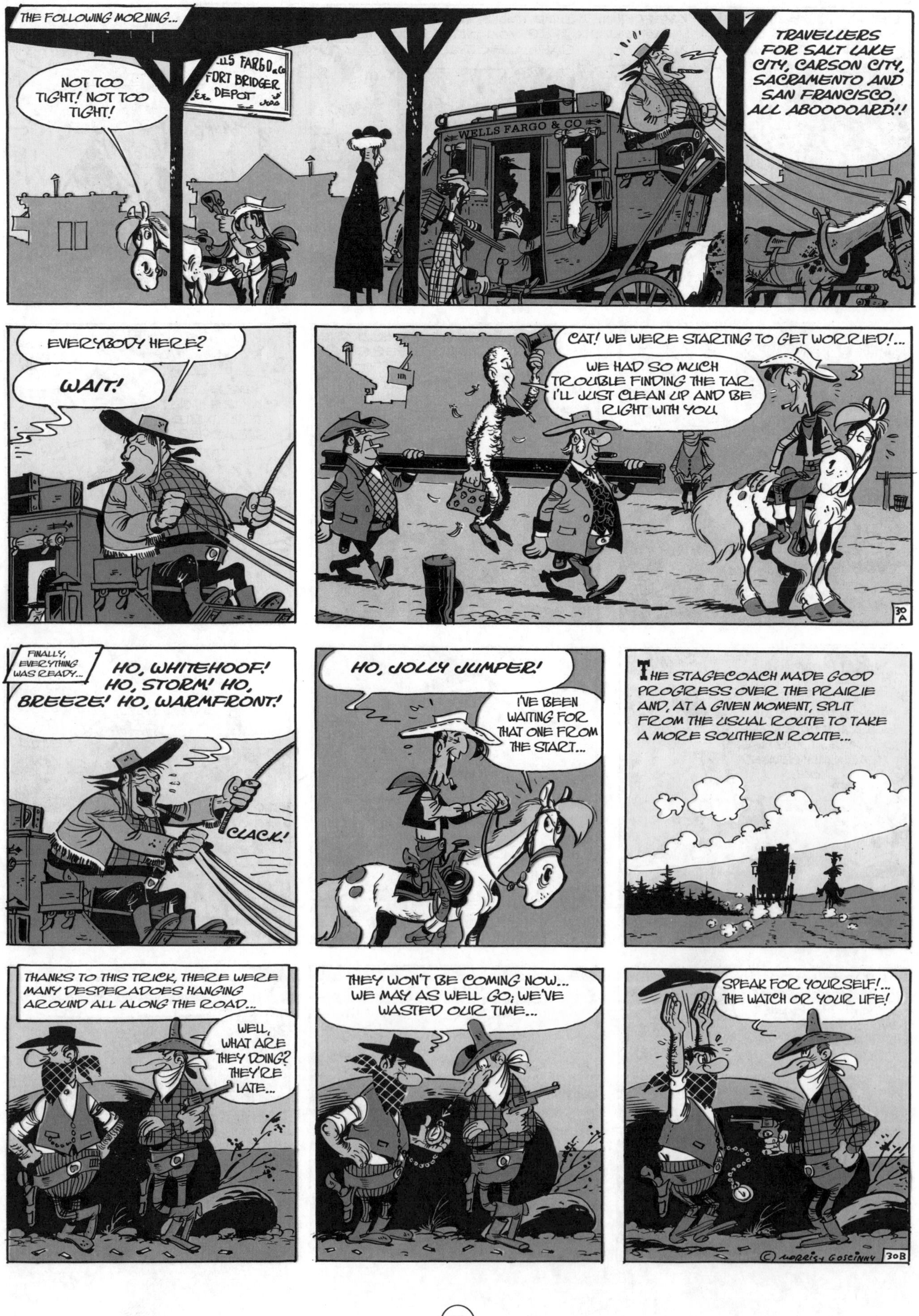
THE FOLLOWING MORNING...
FORT BRIDGER DEPOT
WELLS FARGO & CO
NOT TOO TIGHT! NOT TOO TIGHT!
TRAVELLERS FOR SALT LAKE CITY, CARSON CITY, SACRAMENTO AND SAN FRANCISCO, ALL ABOOOOARD!!
EVERYBODY HERE?
WAIT!
CAT! WE WERE STARTING TO GET WORRIED!...
WE HAD SO MUCH TROUBLE FINDING THE TAR. I'LL JUST CLEAN UP AND BE RIGHT WITH YOU.
FINALLY, EVERYTHING WAS READY...
HO, WHITEHOOF! HO, STORM! HO, BREEZE! HO, WARMFRONT!
CLACK!
HO, JOLLY JUMPER!
I'VE BEEN WAITING FOR THAT ONE FROM THE START...
THE STAGECOACH MADE GOOD PROGRESS OVER THE PRAIRIE AND, AT A GIVEN MOMENT, SPLIT FROM THE USUAL ROUTE TO TAKE A MORE SOUTHERN ROUTE...
THANKS TO THIS TRICK, THERE WERE MANY DESPERADOES HANGING AROUND ALL ALONG THE ROAD...
WELL, WHAT ARE THEY DOING? THEY'RE LATE...
THEY WON'T BE COMING NOW... WE MAY AS WELL GO; WE'VE WASTED OUR TIME...
SPEAK FOR YOURSELF!... THE WATCH OR YOUR LIFE!
© MORRIS+GOSCINNY

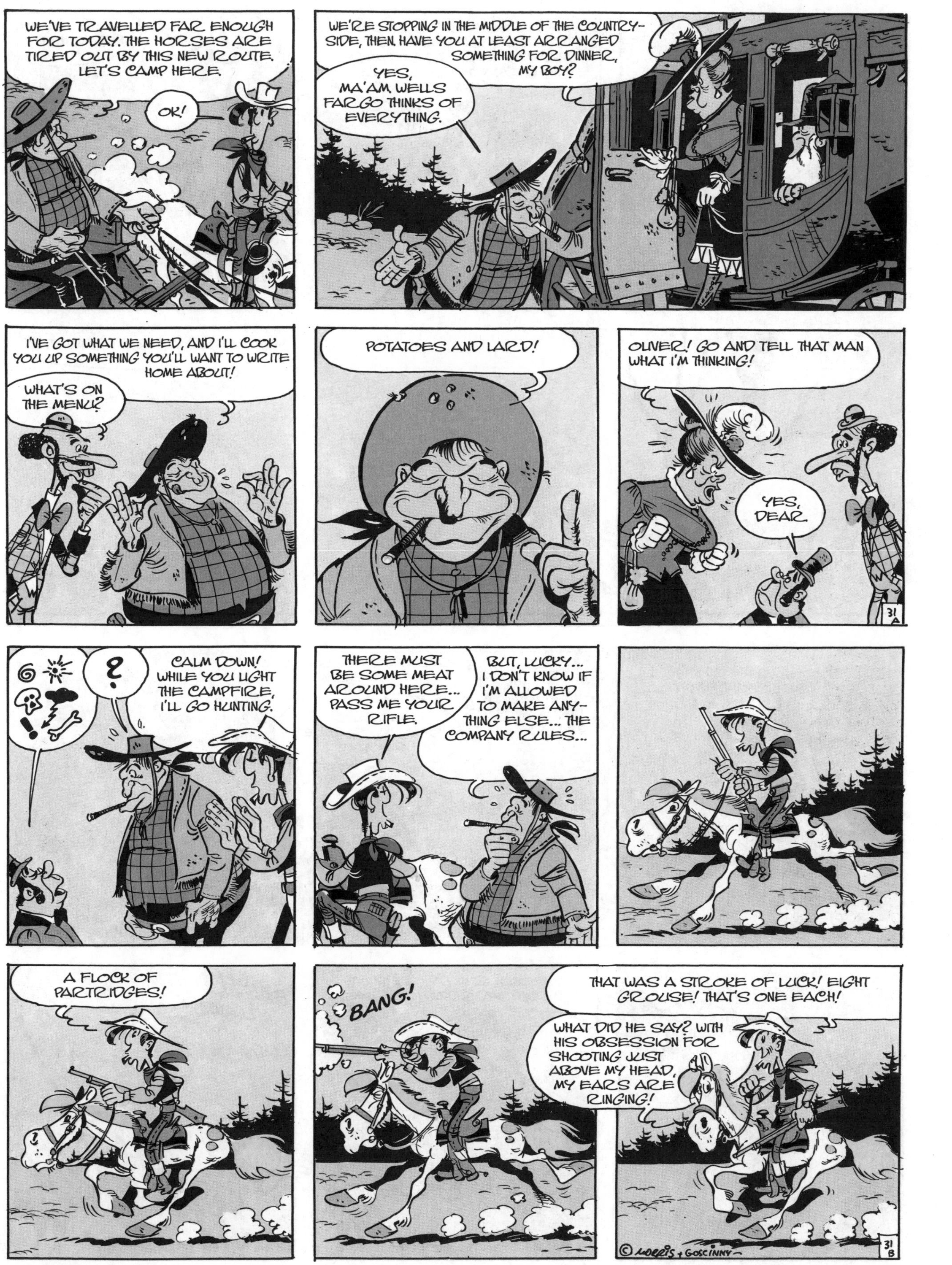
WE'VE TRAVELLED FAR ENOUGH FOR TODAY. THE HORSES ARE TIRED OUT BY THIS NEW ROUTE. LET'S CAMP HERE.
OK!
WE'RE STOPPING IN THE MIDDLE OF THE COUNTRYSIDE, THEN. HAVE YOU AT LEAST ARRANGED SOMETHING FOR DINNER, MY BOY?
YES, MA'AM. WELLS FARGO THINKS OF EVERYTHING.
I'VE GOT WHAT WE NEED, AND I'LL COOK YOU UP SOMETHING YOU'LL WANT TO WRITE HOME ABOUT!
WHAT'S ON THE MENU?
POTATOES AND LARD!
OLIVER! GO AND TELL THAT MAN WHAT I'M THINKING!
YES, DEAR.
31 A
?
CALM DOWN! WHILE YOU LIGHT THE CAMPFIRE, I'LL GO HUNTING.
THERE MUST BE SOME MEAT AROUND HERE... PASS ME YOUR RIFLE.
BUT, LUCKY... I DON'T KNOW IF I'M ALLOWED TO MAKE ANYTHING ELSE... THE COMPANY RULES...
A FLOCK OF PARTRIDGES!
BANG!
THAT WAS A STROKE OF LUCK! EIGHT GROUSE! THAT'S ONE EACH!
WHAT DID HE SAY? WITH HIS OBSESSION FOR SHOOTING JUST ABOVE MY HEAD, MY EARS ARE RINGING!
© MORRIS + GOSCINNY
31 B

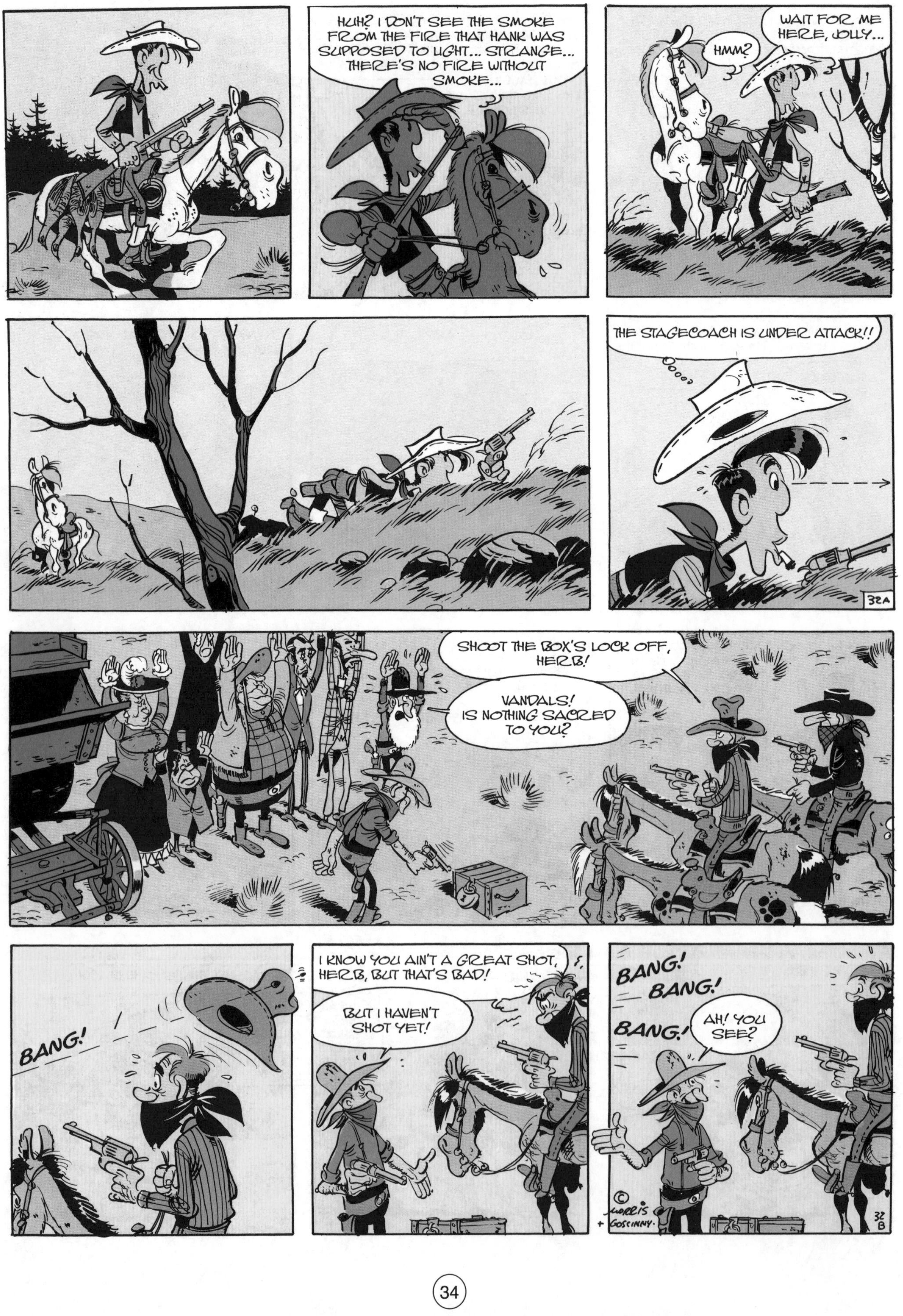
HUH? I DON'T SEE THE SMOKE FROM THE FIRE THAT HANK WAS SUPPOSED TO LIGHT... STRANGE... THERE'S NO FIRE WITHOUT SMOKE...
WAIT FOR ME HERE, JOLLY...
HMM?
THE STAGECOACH IS UNDER ATTACK!!
32A
SHOOT THE BOX'S LOCK OFF, HERB!
VANDALS! IS NOTHING SACRED TO YOU?
BANG!
I KNOW YOU AIN'T A GREAT SHOT, HERB, BUT THAT'S BAD!
BUT I HAVEN'T SHOT YET!
BANG!
BANG!
BANG!
AH! YOU SEE?
© MORRIS + GOSCINNY.
32 B

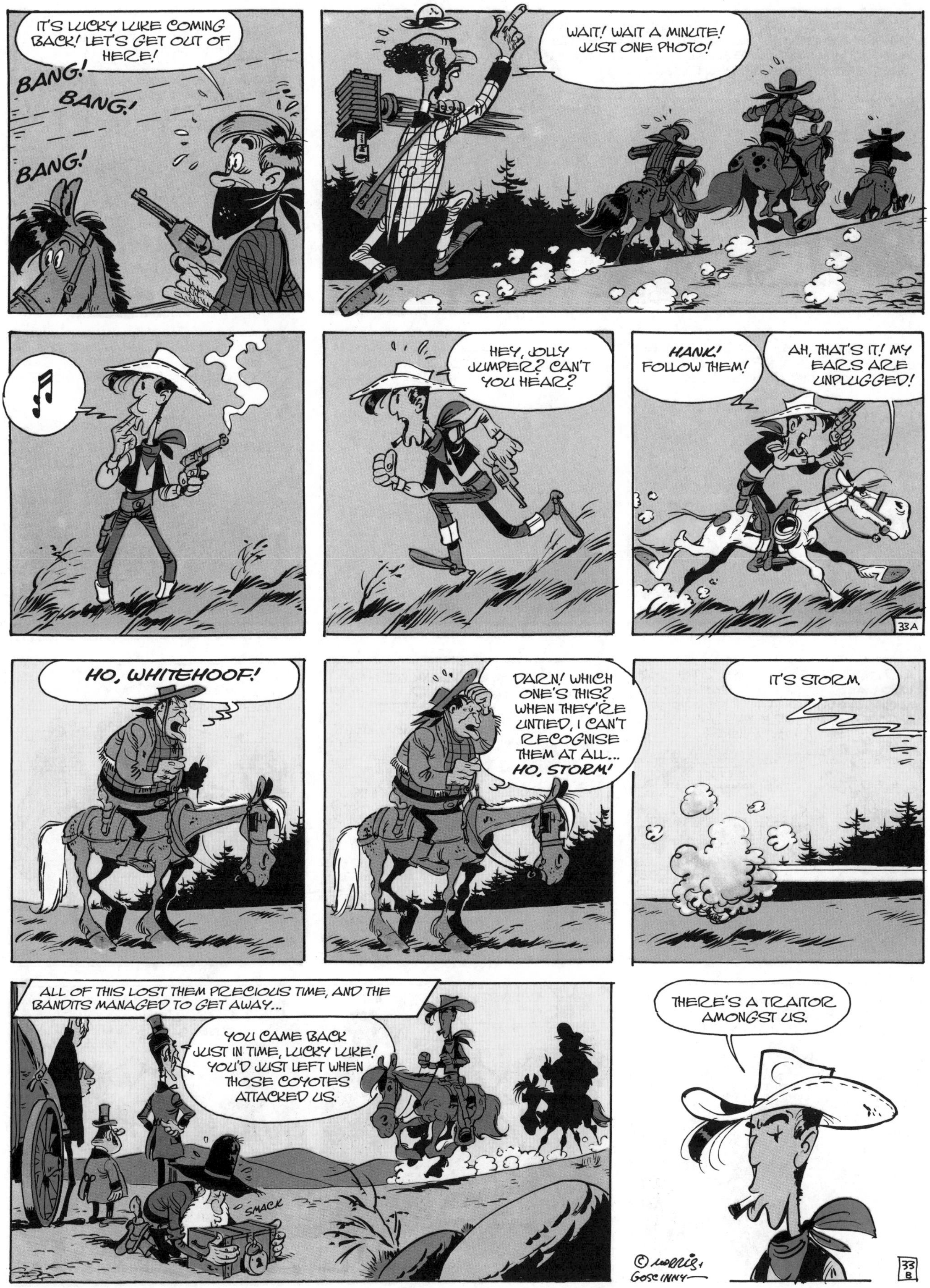

IT'S LUCKY LUKE COMING BACK! LET'S GET OUT OF HERE!
BANG!
BANG!
BANG!
WAIT! WAIT A MINUTE! JUST ONE PHOTO!
HEY, JOLLY JUMPER? CAN'T YOU HEAR?
HANK! FOLLOW THEM!
AH, THAT'S IT! MY EARS ARE UNPLUGGED!
33A
HO, WHITEHOOF!
DARN! WHICH ONE'S THIS? WHEN THEY'RE UNTIED, I CAN'T RECOGNISE THEM AT ALL... HO, STORM!
IT'S STORM.
ALL OF THIS LOST THEM PRECIOUS TIME, AND THE BANDITS MANAGED TO GET AWAY...
YOU CAME BACK JUST IN TIME, LUCKY LUKE! YOU'D JUST LEFT WHEN THOSE COYOTES ATTACKED US.
SMACK
THERE'S A TRAITOR AMONGST US.
© MORRIS + GOSCINNY
33 B

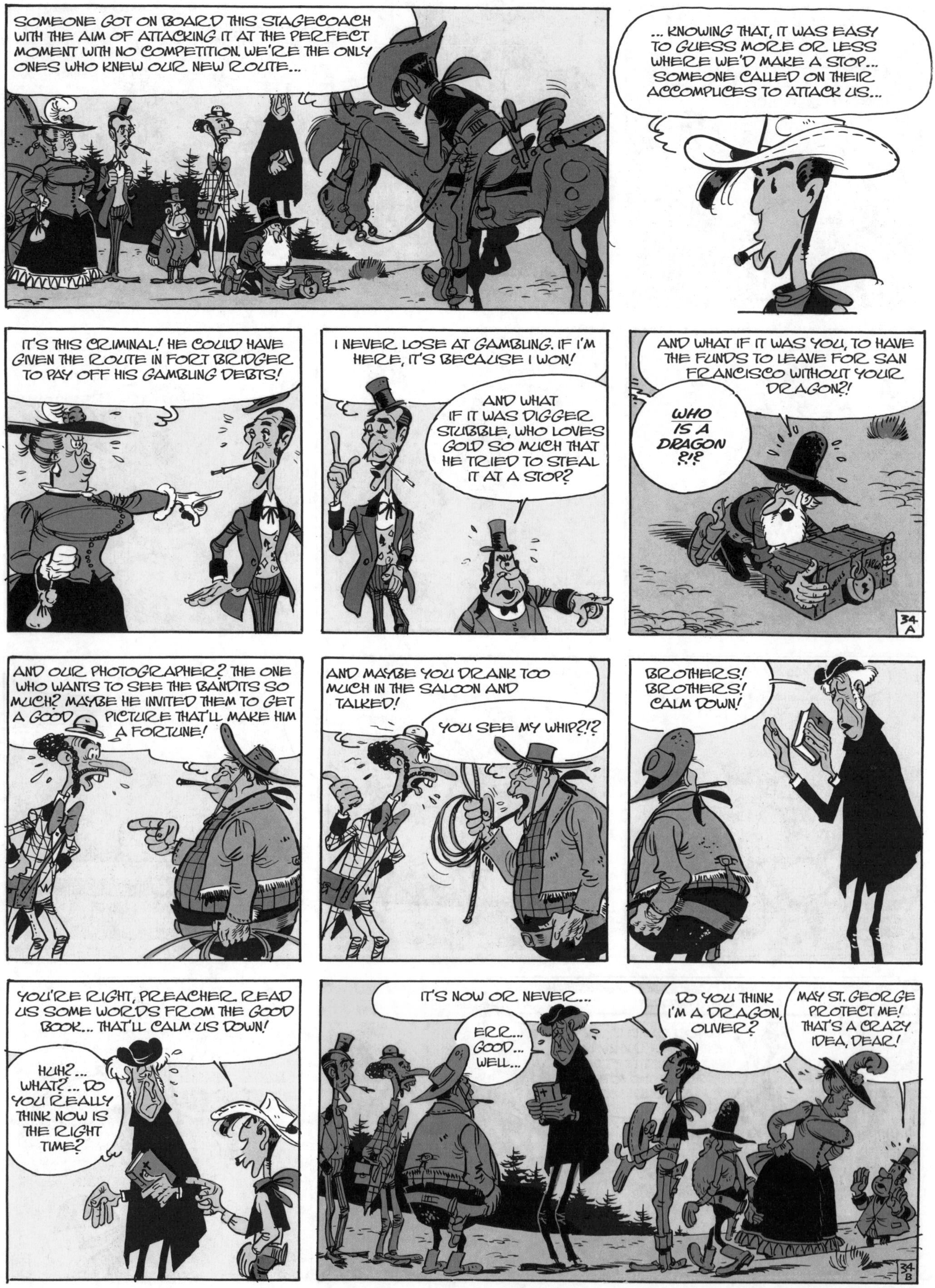
SOMEONE GOT ON BOARD THIS STAGECOACH WITH THE AIM OF ATTACKING IT AT THE PERFECT MOMENT WITH NO COMPETITION. WE'RE THE ONLY ONES WHO KNEW OUR NEW ROUTE...
... KNOWING THAT, IT WAS EASY TO GUESS MORE OR LESS WHERE WE'D MAKE A STOP... SOMEONE CALLED ON THEIR ACCOMPLICES TO ATTACK US...
IT'S THIS CRIMINAL! HE COULD HAVE GIVEN THE ROUTE IN FORT BRIDGER TO PAY OFF HIS GAMBLING DEBTS!
I NEVER LOSE AT GAMBLING. IF I'M HERE, IT'S BECAUSE I WON!
AND WHAT IF IT WAS DIGGER STUBBLE, WHO LOVES GOLD SO MUCH THAT HE TRIED TO STEAL IT AT A STOP?
AND WHAT IF IT WAS YOU, TO HAVE THE FUNDS TO LEAVE FOR SAN FRANCISCO WITHOUT YOUR DRAGON?!
WHO IS A DRAGON ?!?
WELLS FARGO
34 A
AND OUR PHOTOGRAPHER? THE ONE WHO WANTS TO SEE THE BANDITS SO MUCH? MAYBE HE INVITED THEM TO GET A GOOD PICTURE THAT'LL MAKE HIM A FORTUNE!
AND MAYBE YOU DRANK TOO MUCH IN THE SALOON AND TALKED!
YOU SEE MY WHIP?!?
BROTHERS! BROTHERS! CALM DOWN!
YOU'RE RIGHT, PREACHER. READ US SOME WORDS FROM THE GOOD BOOK... THAT'LL CALM US DOWN!
HUH?... WHAT?... DO YOU REALLY THINK NOW IS THE RIGHT TIME?
IT'S NOW OR NEVER...
ERR... GOOD... WELL...
DO YOU THINK I'M A DRAGON, OLIVER?
MAY ST. GEORGE PROTECT ME! THAT'S A CRAZY IDEA, DEAR!
34 B

WELL, REVEREND, WE'RE WAITING...

YES, YES... I'M GATHERING MY THOUGHTS...

ERM... THOU SHALT NOT PLAY CARDS WITH A FALSE DECK... THOU SHALT NOT STEAL HORSES IF YOU DON'T WANT TO BE HANGED HIGH...

... IT'S BETTER TO STEAL FROM RICH THAN POOR...

I'D LIKE TO SEE THAT BOOK UP CLOSE, REVEREND... IT SOUNDS TO ME LIKE IT'S A NEW VERSION...

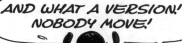

AND WHAT A VERSION! NOBODY MOVE!

CAT! GO TO LUKE AND REMOVE HIS GUN BELT!...

I'M NO MORE OF A PREACHER THAN YOU! FROM THE START, MY MEN AND I HAVE BEEN WAITING FOR THE RIGHT MOMENT TO MAKE OFF WITH THAT GOLD!... I'LL FINISH YOU, LUKE!

GIVE ME YOUR HAND, LUKE...

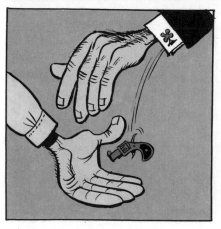

BANG!

!

MISSED!! THE FAMOUS LUCKY LUKE MISSED! THAT WAS YOUR LAST SHOT, LUKE!

MORRIS + GOSCINNY

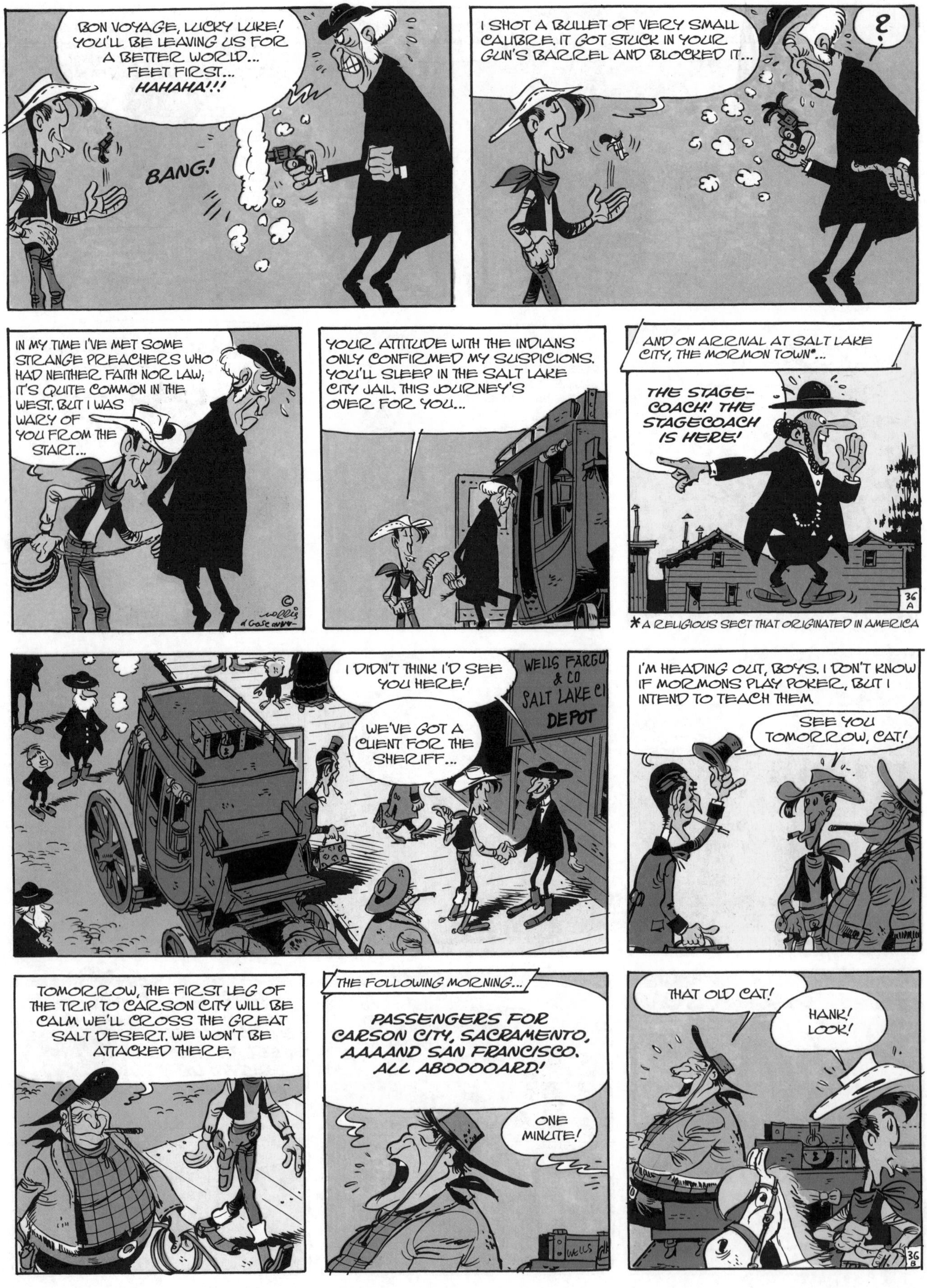

BON VOYAGE, LUCKY LUKE! YOU'LL BE LEAVING US FOR A BETTER WORLD... FEET FIRST... HAHAHA!!!
BANG!
I SHOT A BULLET OF VERY SMALL CALIBRE. IT GOT STUCK IN YOUR GUN'S BARREL AND BLOCKED IT...
?
IN MY TIME I'VE MET SOME STRANGE PREACHERS WHO HAD NEITHER FAITH NOR LAW; IT'S QUITE COMMON IN THE WEST. BUT I WAS WARY OF YOU FROM THE START...
YOUR ATTITUDE WITH THE INDIANS ONLY CONFIRMED MY SUSPICIONS. YOU'LL SLEEP IN THE SALT LAKE CITY JAIL. THIS JOURNEY'S OVER FOR YOU...
AND ON ARRIVAL AT SALT LAKE CITY, THE MORMON TOWN*...
THE STAGE-COACH! THE STAGECOACH IS HERE!
* A RELIGIOUS SECT THAT ORIGINATED IN AMERICA
WELLS FARGO & CO SALT LAKE CI DEPOT
I DIDN'T THINK I'D SEE YOU HERE!
WE'VE GOT A CLIENT FOR THE SHERIFF...
I'M HEADING OUT, BOYS. I DON'T KNOW IF MORMONS PLAY POKER, BUT I INTEND TO TEACH THEM.
SEE YOU TOMORROW, CAT!
TOMORROW, THE FIRST LEG OF THE TRIP TO CARSON CITY WILL BE CALM. WE'LL CROSS THE GREAT SALT DESERT. WE WON'T BE ATTACKED THERE.
THE FOLLOWING MORNING...
PASSENGERS FOR CARSON CITY, SACRAMENTO, AAAAND SAN FRANCISCO. ALL ABOOOOARD!
ONE MINUTE!
THAT OLD CAT!
HANK! LOOK!

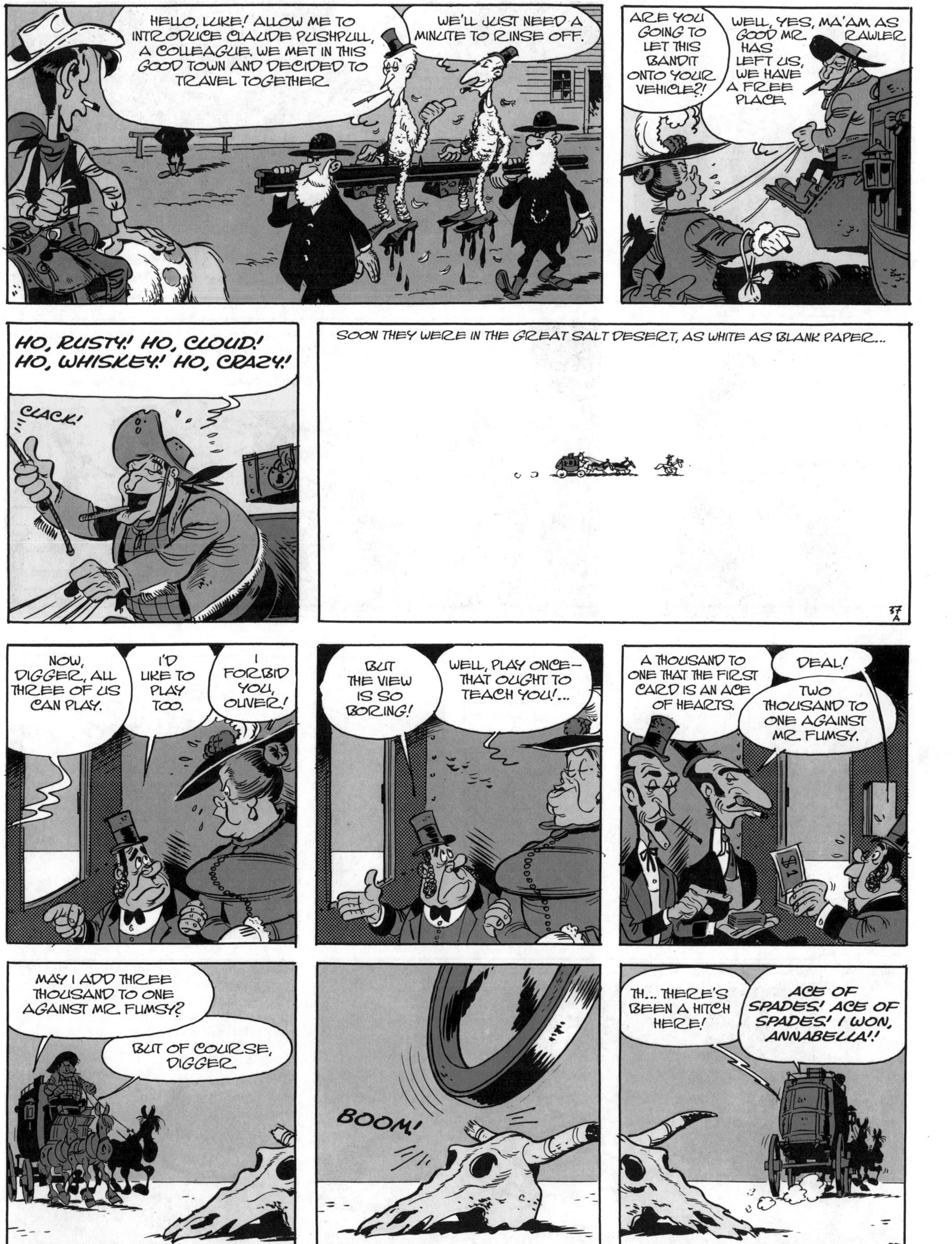
HELLO, LUKE! ALLOW ME TO INTRODUCE CLAUDE PUSHPULL, A COLLEAGUE. WE MET IN THIS GOOD TOWN AND DECIDED TO TRAVEL TOGETHER.
WE'LL JUST NEED A MINUTE TO RINSE OFF.
ARE YOU GOING TO LET THIS BANDIT ONTO YOUR VEHICLE?!
WELL, YES, MA'AM. AS GOOD MR. RAWLER HAS LEFT US, WE HAVE A FREE PLACE.
HO, RUSTY! HO, CLOUD! HO, WHISKEY! HO, CRAZY!
CLACK!
SOON THEY WERE IN THE GREAT SALT DESERT, AS WHITE AS BLANK PAPER...
37 A
NOW, DIGGER, ALL THREE OF US CAN PLAY.
I'D LIKE TO PLAY TOO.
I FORBID YOU, OLIVER!
BUT THE VIEW IS SO BORING!
WELL, PLAY ONCE— THAT OUGHT TO TEACH YOU!...
A THOUSAND TO ONE THAT THE FIRST CARD IS AN ACE OF HEARTS.
DEAL!
TWO THOUSAND TO ONE AGAINST MR. FUMSY.
MAY I ADD THREE THOUSAND TO ONE AGAINST MR. FUMSY?
BUT OF COURSE, DIGGER.
BOOM!
TH... THERE'S BEEN A HITCH HERE!
ACE OF SPADES! ACE OF SPADES! I WON, ANNABELLA!!
© MORRIS + GOSCINNY
37 B

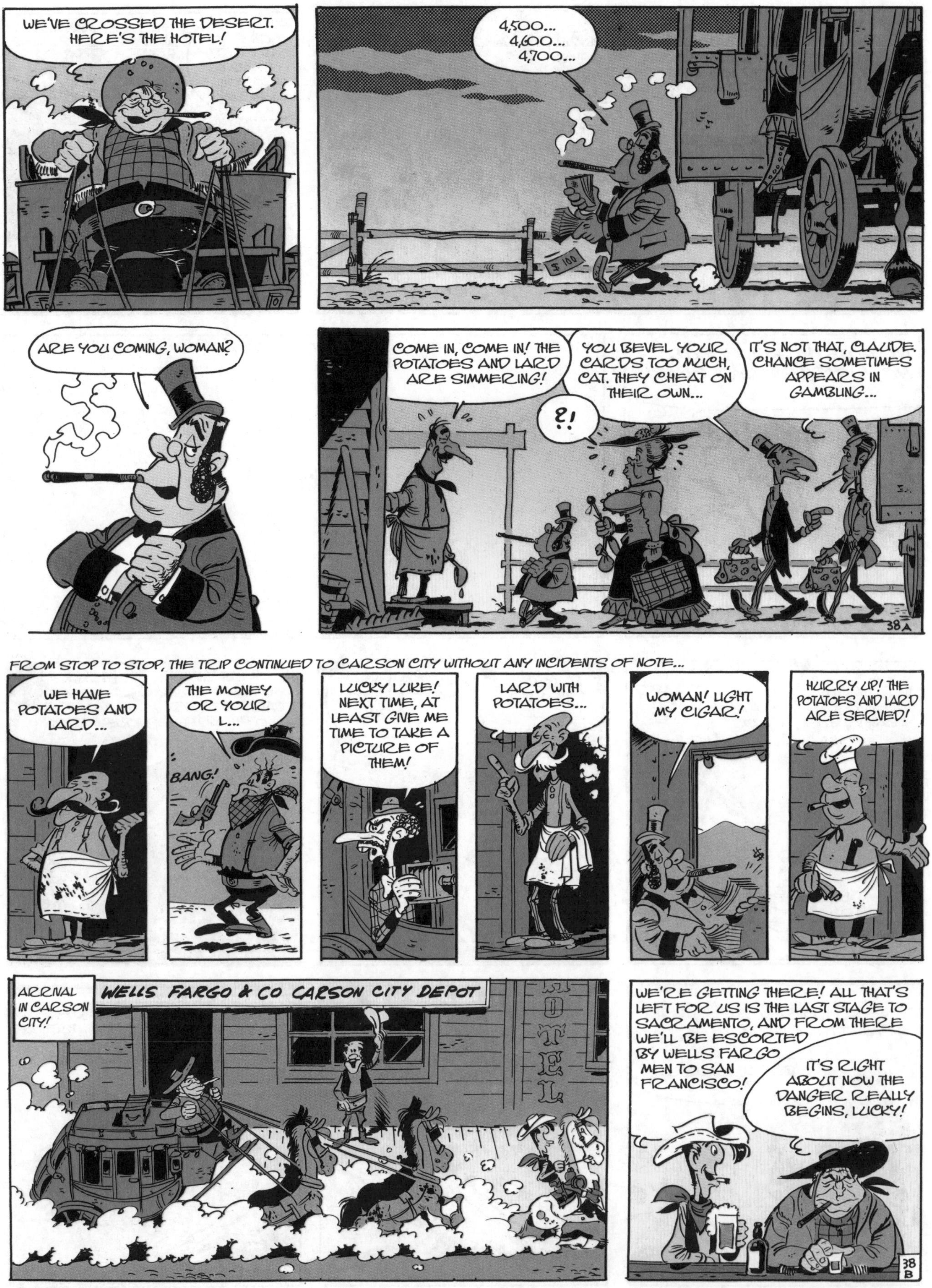

WE'VE CROSSED THE DESERT. HERE'S THE HOTEL!
4,500... 4,600... 4,700...
$ 100
ARE YOU COMING, WOMAN?
COME IN, COME IN! THE POTATOES AND LARD ARE SIMMERING!
YOU BEVEL YOUR CARDS TOO MUCH, CAT. THEY CHEAT ON THEIR OWN...
?!
IT'S NOT THAT, CLAUDE. CHANCE SOMETIMES APPEARS IN GAMBLING...
38 A
FROM STOP TO STOP, THE TRIP CONTINUED TO CARSON CITY WITHOUT ANY INCIDENTS OF NOTE...
WE HAVE POTATOES AND LARD...
THE MONEY OR YOUR L...
BANG!
LUCKY LUKE! NEXT TIME, AT LEAST GIVE ME TIME TO TAKE A PICTURE OF THEM!
LARD WITH POTATOES...
WOMAN! LIGHT MY CIGAR!
HURRY UP! THE POTATOES AND LARD ARE SERVED!
ARRIVAL IN CARSON CITY!
WELLS FARGO & CO CARSON CITY DEPOT
HOTEL
WE'RE GETTING THERE! ALL THAT'S LEFT FOR US IS THE LAST STAGE TO SACRAMENTO, AND FROM THERE WE'LL BE ESCORTED BY WELLS FARGO MEN TO SAN FRANCISCO!
IT'S RIGHT ABOUT NOW THE DANGER REALLY BEGINS, LUCKY!
38 B

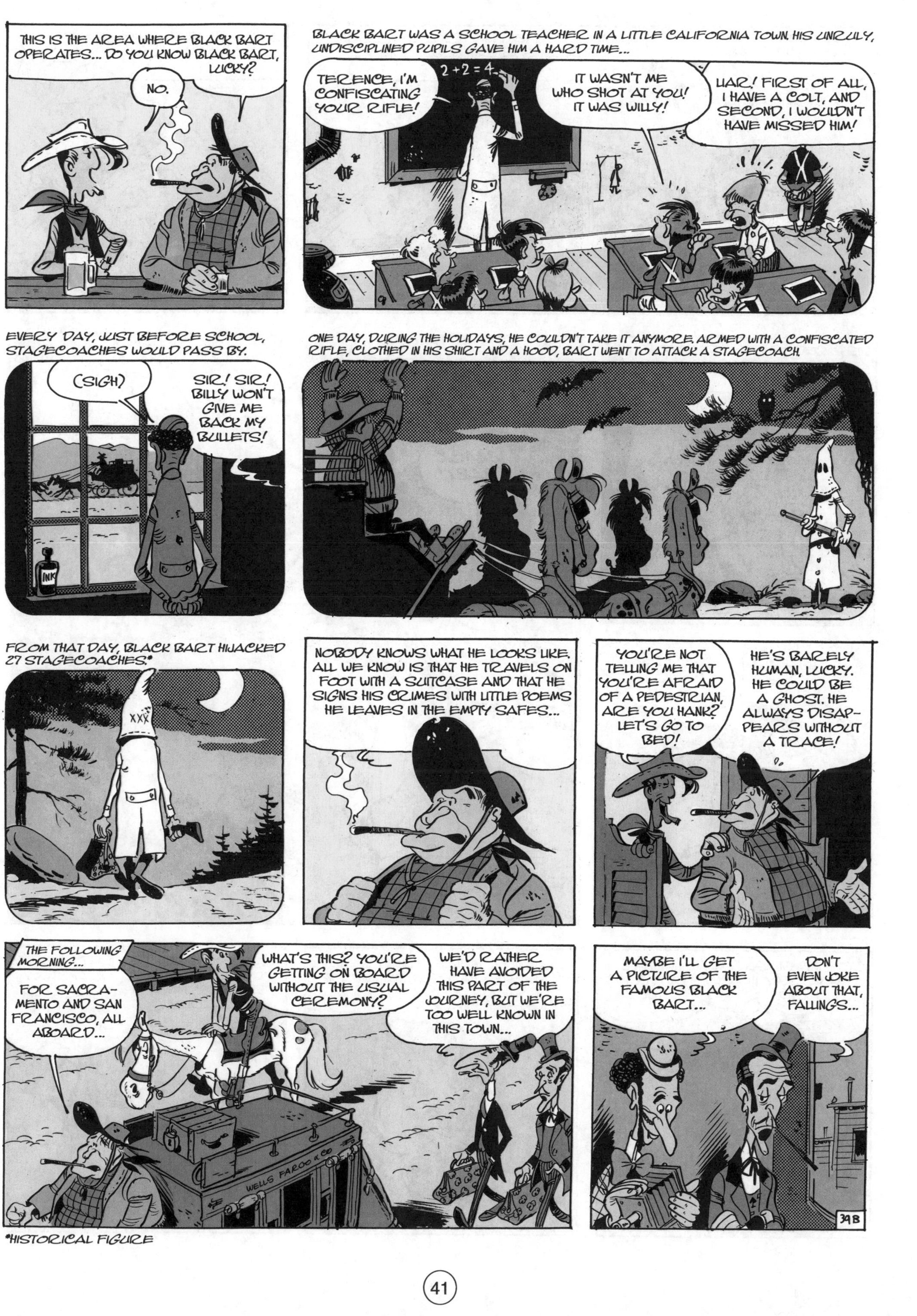
THIS IS THE AREA WHERE BLACK BART OPERATES... DO YOU KNOW BLACK BART, LUCKY?
NO.
BLACK BART WAS A SCHOOL TEACHER IN A LITTLE CALIFORNIA TOWN. HIS UNRULY, UNDISCIPLINED PUPILS GAVE HIM A HARD TIME...
2 + 2 = 4
TERENCE, I'M CONFISCATING YOUR RIFLE!
IT WASN'T ME WHO SHOT AT YOU! IT WAS WILLY!
LIAR! FIRST OF ALL, I HAVE A COLT, AND SECOND, I WOULDN'T HAVE MISSED HIM!
EVERY DAY, JUST BEFORE SCHOOL, STAGECOACHES WOULD PASS BY.
(SIGH)
SIR! SIR! BILLY WON'T GIVE ME BACK MY BULLETS!
INK
ONE DAY, DURING THE HOLIDAYS, HE COULDN'T TAKE IT ANYMORE. ARMED WITH A CONFISCATED RIFLE, CLOTHED IN HIS SHIRT AND A HOOD, BART WENT TO ATTACK A STAGECOACH.
FROM THAT DAY, BLACK BART HIJACKED 27 STAGECOACHES.*
XXX
NOBODY KNOWS WHAT HE LOOKS LIKE. ALL WE KNOW IS THAT HE TRAVELS ON FOOT WITH A SUITCASE AND THAT HE SIGNS HIS CRIMES WITH LITTLE POEMS HE LEAVES IN THE EMPTY SAFES...
YOU'RE NOT TELLING ME THAT YOU'RE AFRAID OF A PEDESTRIAN, ARE YOU HANK? LET'S GO TO BED!
HE'S BARELY HUMAN, LUCKY. HE COULD BE A GHOST. HE ALWAYS DISAPPEARS WITHOUT A TRACE!
THE FOLLOWING MORNING...
FOR SACRAMENTO AND SAN FRANCISCO, ALL ABOARD...
WHAT'S THIS? YOU'RE GETTING ON BOARD WITHOUT THE USUAL CEREMONY?
WE'D RATHER HAVE AVOIDED THIS PART OF THE JOURNEY, BUT WE'RE TOO WELL KNOWN IN THIS TOWN...
WELLS FARGO & CO
MAYBE I'LL GET A PICTURE OF THE FAMOUS BLACK BART...
DON'T EVEN JOKE ABOUT THAT, FALLINGS...
39B

*HISTORICAL FIGURE

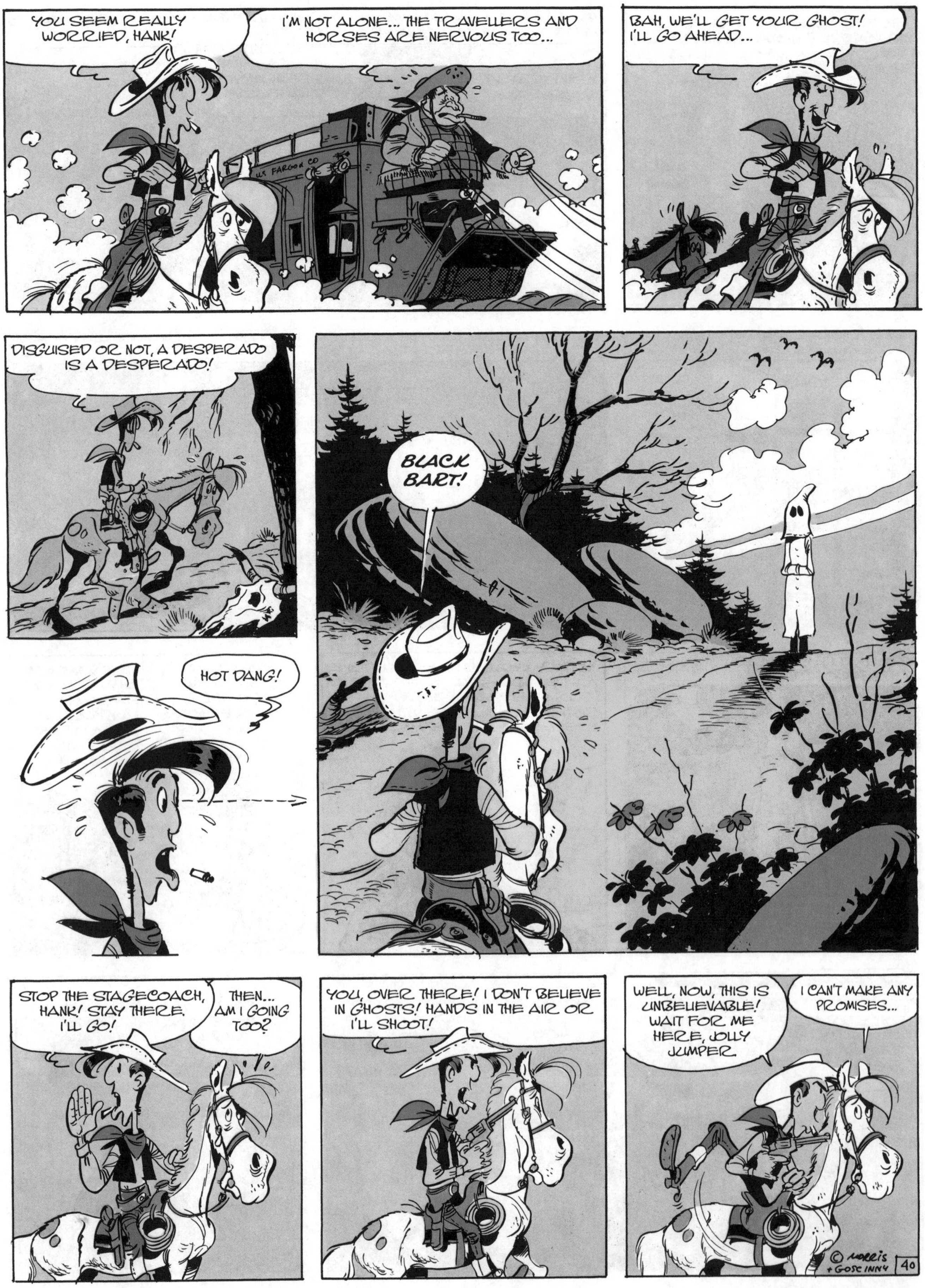
YOU SEEM REALLY WORRIED, HANK!
I'M NOT ALONE... THE TRAVELLERS AND HORSES ARE NERVOUS TOO...
BAH, WE'LL GET YOUR GHOST! I'LL GO AHEAD...
DISGUISED OR NOT, A DESPERADO IS A DESPERADO!
HOT DANG!
BLACK BART!
STOP THE STAGECOACH, HANK! STAY THERE. I'LL GO!
THEN... AM I GOING TOO?
YOU, OVER THERE! I DON'T BELIEVE IN GHOSTS! HANDS IN THE AIR OR I'LL SHOOT!
WELL, NOW, THIS IS UNBELIEVABLE! WAIT FOR ME HERE, JOLLY JUMPER.
I CAN'T MAKE ANY PROMISES...
© MORRIS + GOSCINNY
40

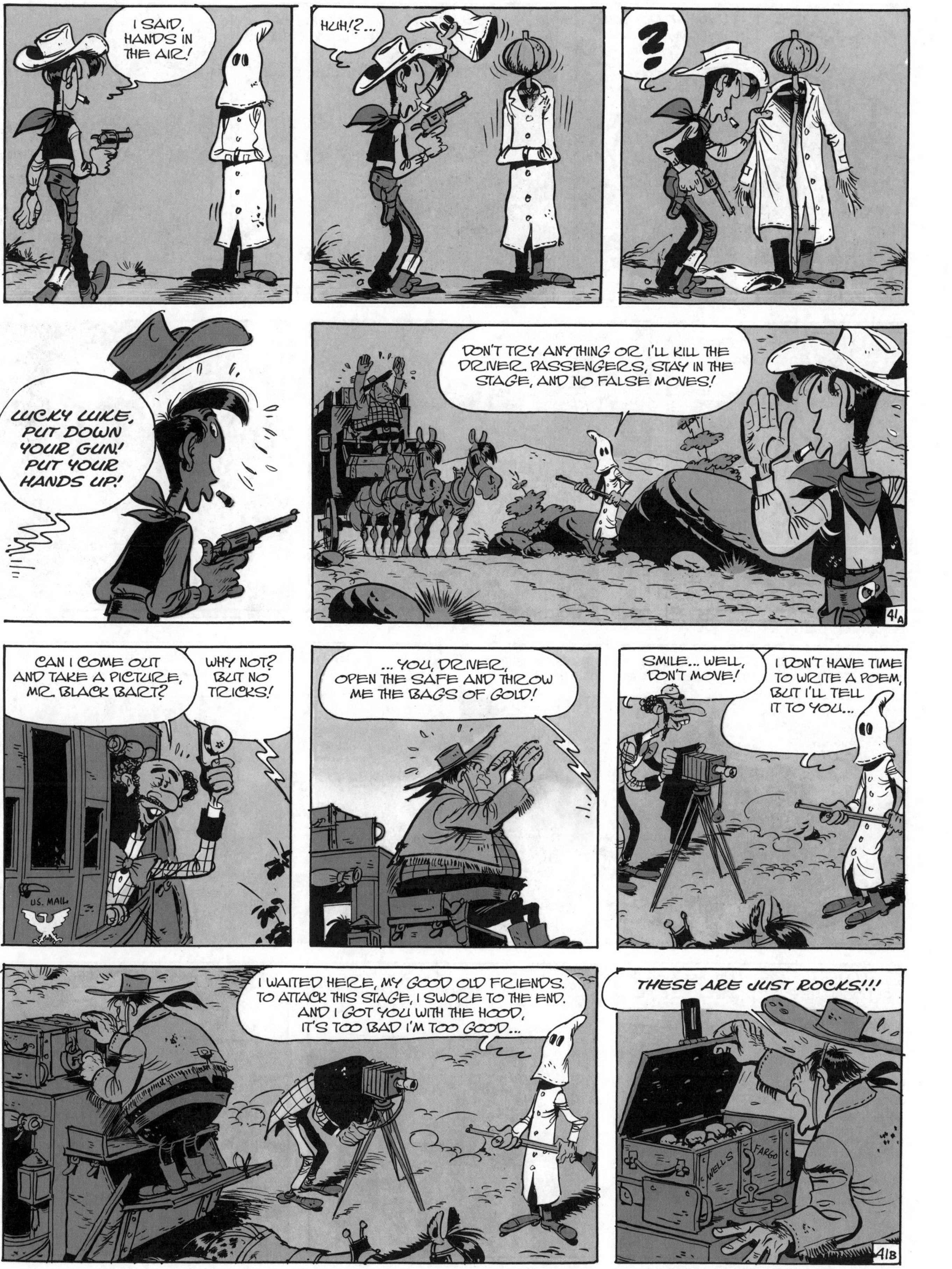

I SAID, HANDS IN THE AIR!
HUH!?...
?
LUCKY LUKE, PUT DOWN YOUR GUN! PUT YOUR HANDS UP!
DON'T TRY ANYTHING OR I'LL KILL THE DRIVER. PASSENGERS, STAY IN THE STAGE, AND NO FALSE MOVES!
41A
CAN I COME OUT AND TAKE A PICTURE, MR. BLACK BART?
WHY NOT? BUT NO TRICKS!
U.S. MAIL
... YOU, DRIVER, OPEN THE SAFE AND THROW ME THE BAGS OF GOLD!
SMILE... WELL, DON'T MOVE!
I DON'T HAVE TIME TO WRITE A POEM, BUT I'LL TELL IT TO YOU...
I WAITED HERE, MY GOOD OLD FRIENDS. TO ATTACK THIS STAGE, I SWORE TO THE END. AND I GOT YOU WITH THE HOOD, IT'S TOO BAD I'M TOO GOOD...
THESE ARE JUST ROCKS!!!
WELLS FARGO
41B

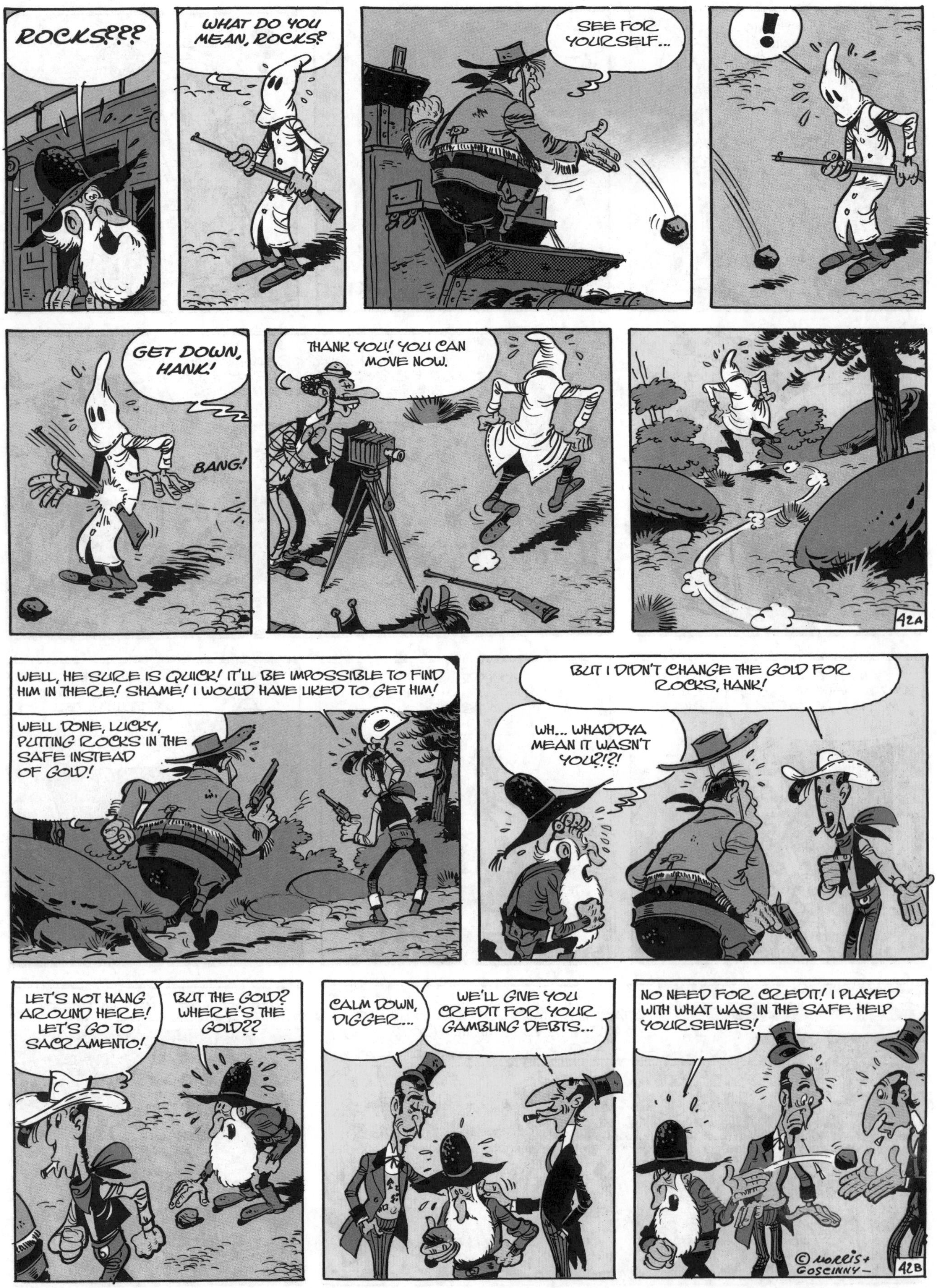
ROCKS???
WHAT DO YOU MEAN, ROCKS?
SEE FOR YOURSELF...
!
GET DOWN, HANK!
BANG!
THANK YOU! YOU CAN MOVE NOW.
42A
WELL, HE SURE IS QUICK! IT'LL BE IMPOSSIBLE TO FIND HIM IN THERE! SHAME! I WOULD HAVE LIKED TO GET HIM!
WELL DONE, LUCKY, PUTTING ROCKS IN THE SAFE INSTEAD OF GOLD!
BUT I DIDN'T CHANGE THE GOLD FOR ROCKS, HANK!
WH... WHADDYA MEAN IT WASN'T YOU?!?!
LET'S NOT HANG AROUND HERE! LET'S GO TO SACRAMENTO!
BUT THE GOLD? WHERE'S THE GOLD??
CALM DOWN, DIGGER...
WE'LL GIVE YOU CREDIT FOR YOUR GAMBLING DEBTS...
NO NEED FOR CREDIT! I PLAYED WITH WHAT WAS IN THE SAFE. HELP YOURSELVES!
© MORRIS + GOSCINNY
42B

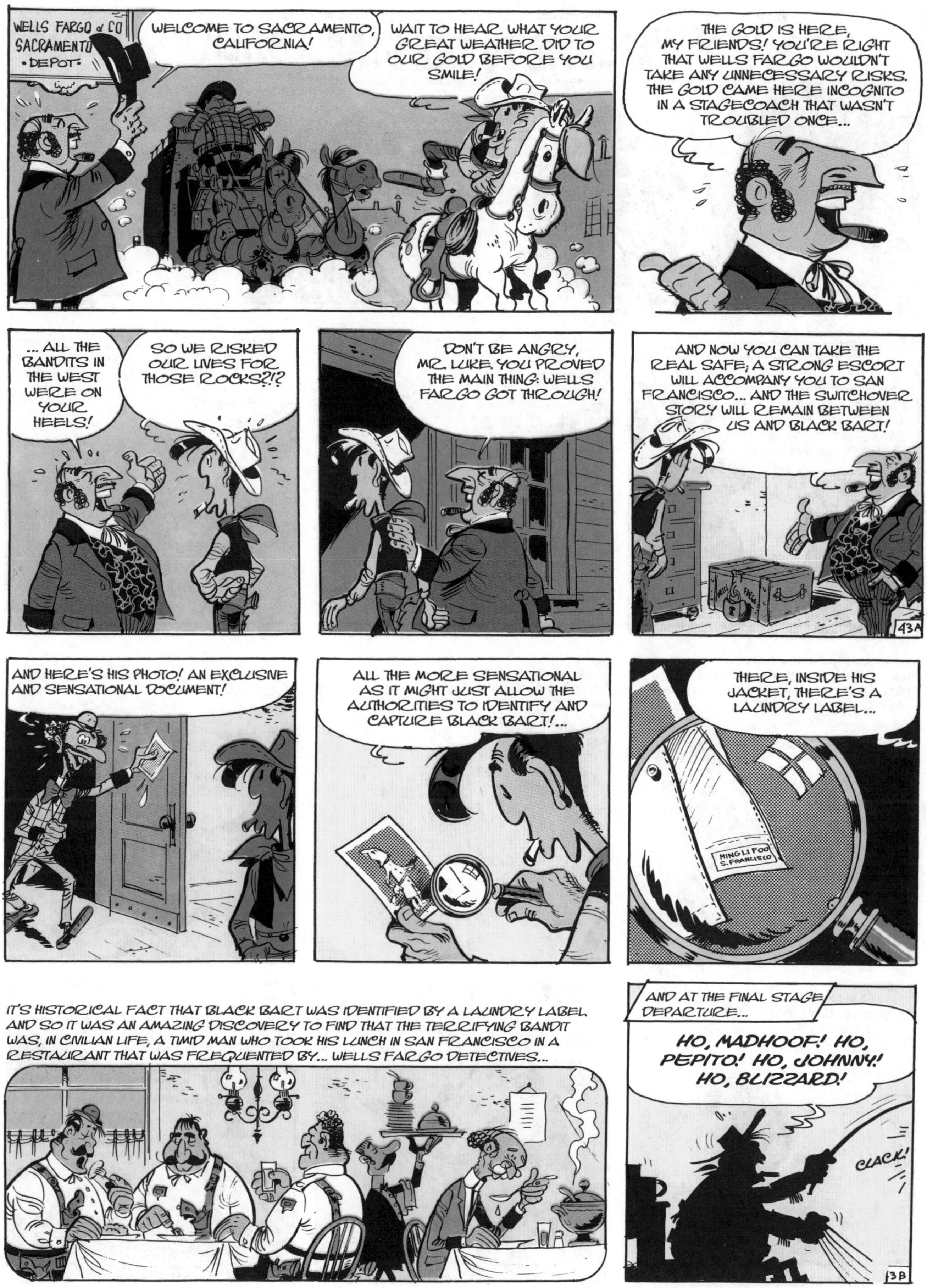

WELLS FARGO & CO SACRAMENTO •DEPOT•
WELCOME TO SACRAMENTO, CALIFORNIA!
WAIT TO HEAR WHAT YOUR GREAT WEATHER DID TO OUR GOLD BEFORE YOU SMILE!
THE GOLD IS HERE, MY FRIENDS! YOU'RE RIGHT THAT WELLS FARGO WOULDN'T TAKE ANY UNNECESSARY RISKS. THE GOLD CAME HERE INCOGNITO IN A STAGECOACH THAT WASN'T TROUBLED ONCE...
... ALL THE BANDITS IN THE WEST WERE ON YOUR HEELS!
SO WE RISKED OUR LIVES FOR THOSE ROCKS?!?
DON'T BE ANGRY, MR. LUKE, YOU PROVED THE MAIN THING: WELLS FARGO GOT THROUGH!
AND NOW YOU CAN TAKE THE REAL SAFE; A STRONG ESCORT WILL ACCOMPANY YOU TO SAN FRANCISCO... AND THE SWITCHOVER STORY WILL REMAIN BETWEEN US AND BLACK BART!
WELLS FARGO
43A
AND HERE'S HIS PHOTO! AN EXCLUSIVE AND SENSATIONAL DOCUMENT!
ALL THE MORE SENSATIONAL AS IT MIGHT JUST ALLOW THE AUTHORITIES TO IDENTIFY AND CAPTURE BLACK BART!...
THERE, INSIDE HIS JACKET, THERE'S A LAUNDRY LABEL...
MING LI FOO S. FRANCISCO
IT'S HISTORICAL FACT THAT BLACK BART WAS IDENTIFIED BY A LAUNDRY LABEL. AND SO IT WAS AN AMAZING DISCOVERY TO FIND THAT THE TERRIFYING BANDIT WAS, IN CIVILIAN LIFE, A TIMID MAN WHO TOOK HIS LUNCH IN SAN FRANCISCO IN A RESTAURANT THAT WAS FREQUENTED BY... WELLS FARGO DETECTIVES...
AND AT THE FINAL STAGE DEPARTURE...
HO, MADHOOF! HO, PEPITO! HO, JOHNNY! HO, BLIZZARD!
CLACK!
13B

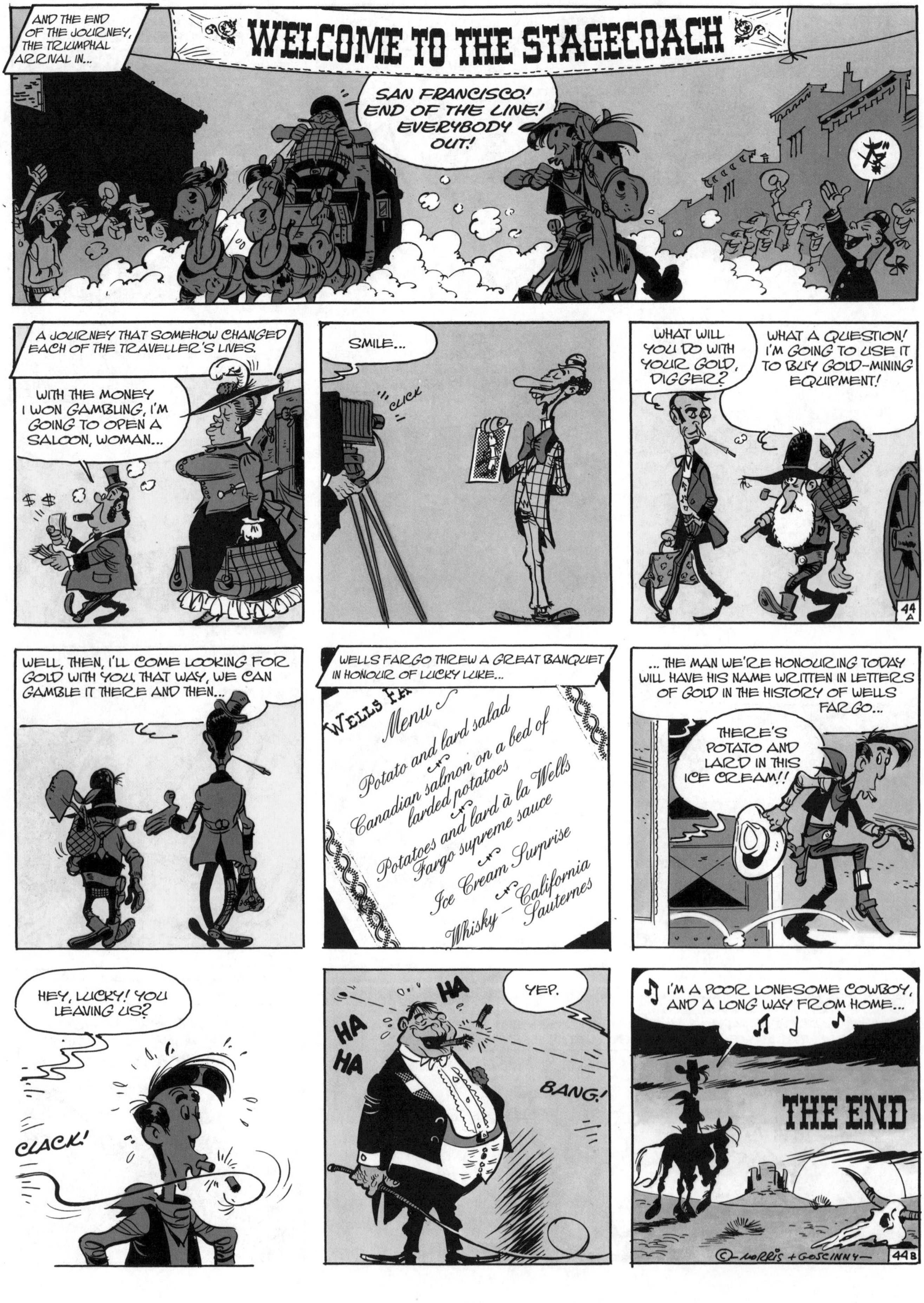
AND THE END OF THE JOURNEY, THE TRIUMPHAL ARRIVAL IN...
WELCOME TO THE STAGECOACH
SAN FRANCISCO! END OF THE LINE! EVERYBODY OUT!
A JOURNEY THAT SOMEHOW CHANGED EACH OF THE TRAVELLER'S LIVES.
WITH THE MONEY I WON GAMBLING, I'M GOING TO OPEN A SALOON, WOMAN...
$ $
SMILE...
CLICK
WHAT WILL YOU DO WITH YOUR GOLD, DIGGER?
WHAT A QUESTION! I'M GOING TO USE IT TO BUY GOLD-MINING EQUIPMENT!
44 A
WELL, THEN, I'LL COME LOOKING FOR GOLD WITH YOU. THAT WAY, WE CAN GAMBLE IT THERE AND THEN...
WELLS FARGO THREW A GREAT BANQUET IN HONOUR OF LUCKY LUKE...
WELLS FA
Menu
Potato and lard salad
Canadian salmon on a bed of larded potatoes
Potatoes and lard à la Wells Fargo supreme sauce
Ice Cream Surprise
Whisky – California Sauternes
... THE MAN WE'RE HONOURING TODAY WILL HAVE HIS NAME WRITTEN IN LETTERS OF GOLD IN THE HISTORY OF WELLS FARGO...
THERE'S POTATO AND LARD IN THIS ICE CREAM!!
HEY, LUCKY! YOU LEAVING US?
CLACK!
HA
HA
HA
YEP.
BANG!
I'M A POOR LONESOME COWBOY, AND A LONG WAY FROM HOME...
THE END
© MORRIS + GOSCINNY
44 B

presents

LUCKY LUKE

The man who shoots faster than his own shadow

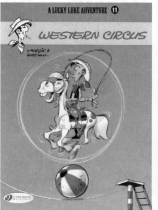

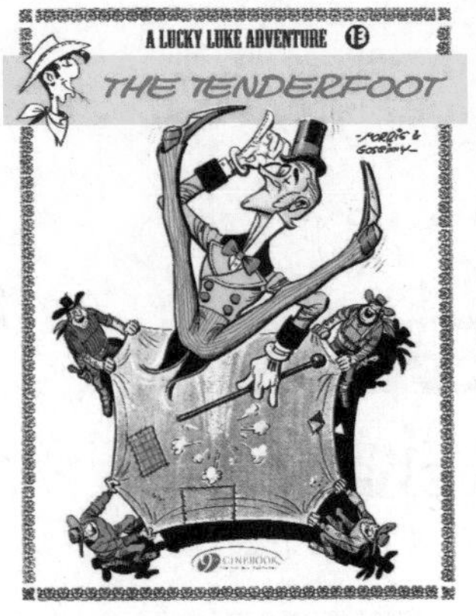
A LUCKY LUKE ADVENTURE 13
THE TENDERFOOT
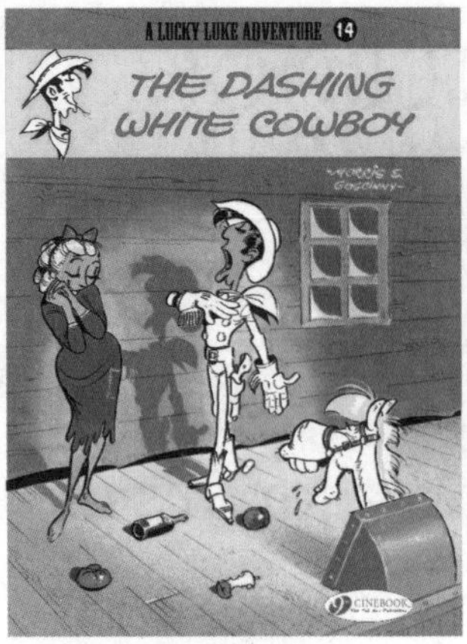
A LUCKY LUKE ADVENTURE 14
THE DASHING WHITE COWBOY
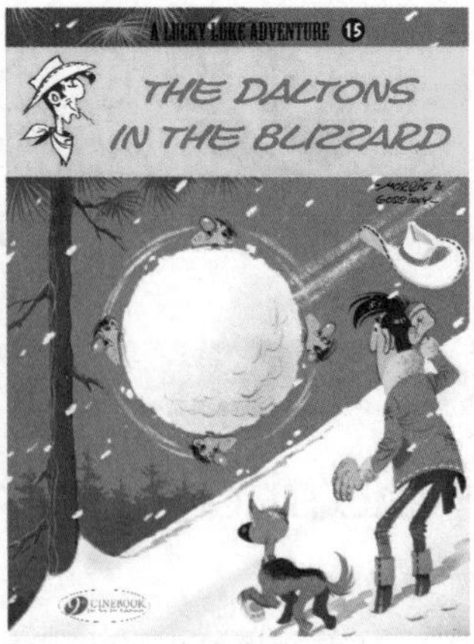
A LUCKY LUKE ADVENTURE 15
THE DALTONS IN THE BLIZZARD
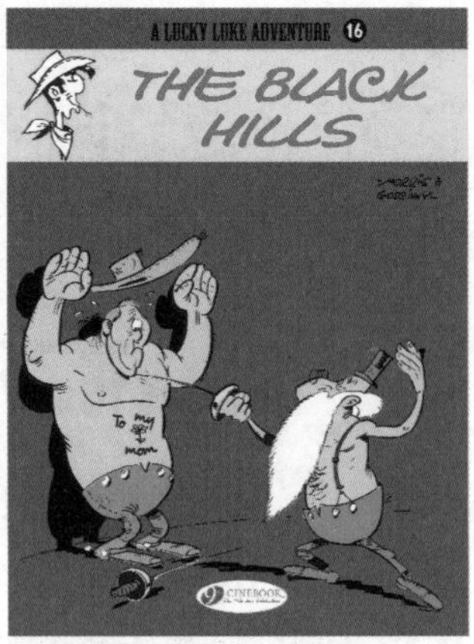
A LUCKY LUKE ADVENTURE 16
THE BLACK HILLS
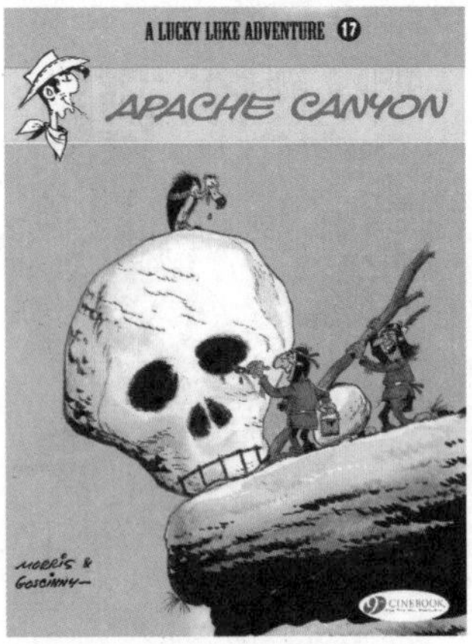
A LUCKY LUKE ADVENTURE 17
APACHE CANYON
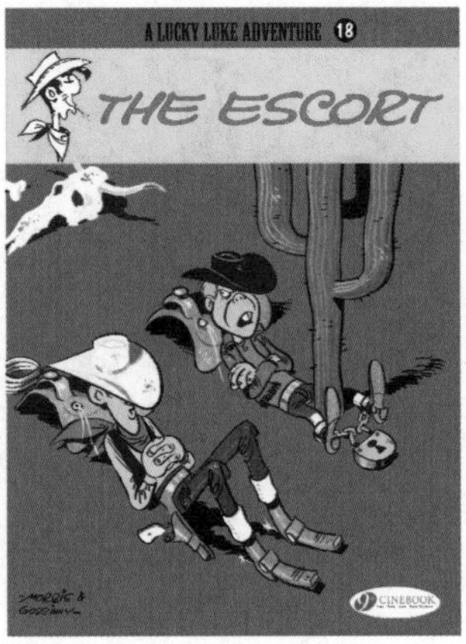
A LUCKY LUKE ADVENTURE 18
THE ESCORT
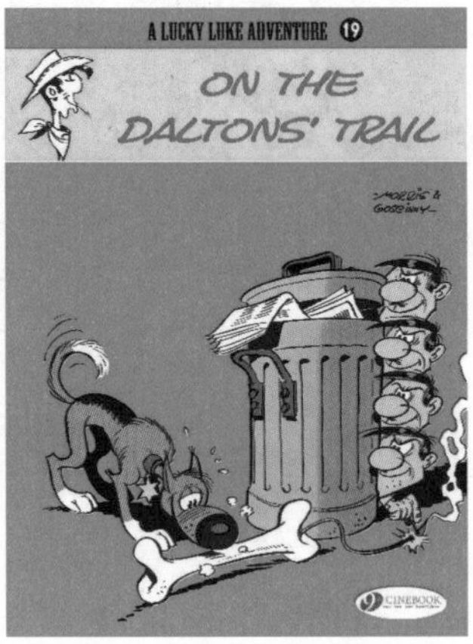
A LUCKY LUKE ADVENTURE 19
ON THE DALTONS' TRAIL
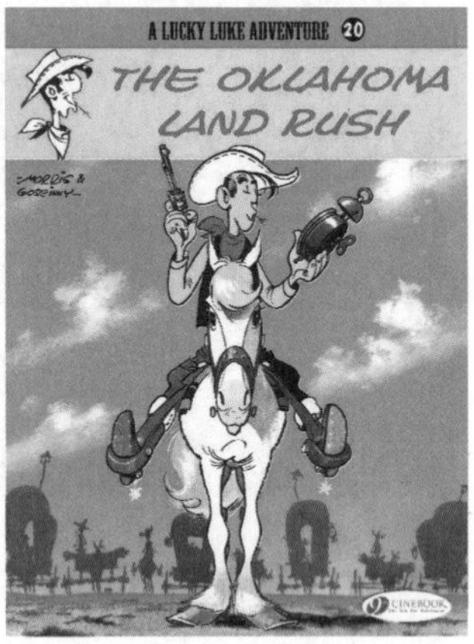
A LUCKY LUKE ADVENTURE 20
THE OKLAHOMA LAND RUSH
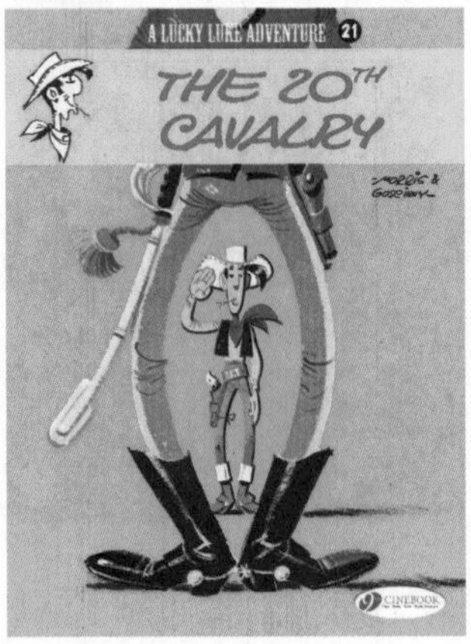
A LUCKY LUKE ADVENTURE 21
THE 20TH CAVALRY
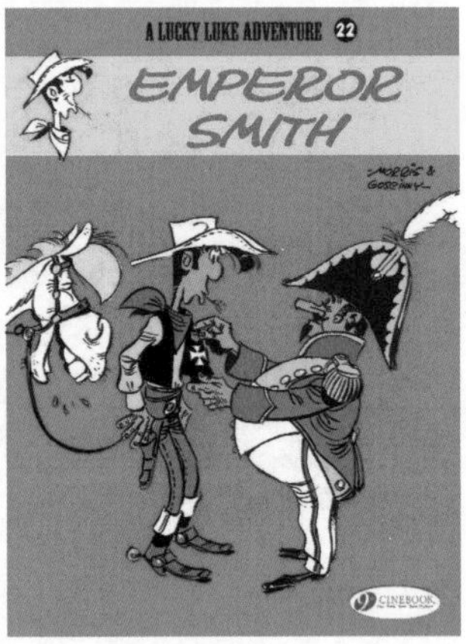
A LUCKY LUKE ADVENTURE 22
EMPEROR SMITH
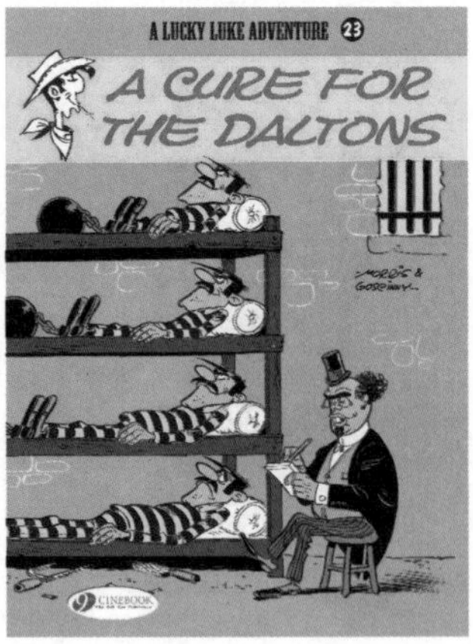
A LUCKY LUKE ADVENTURE 23
A CURE FOR THE DALTONS
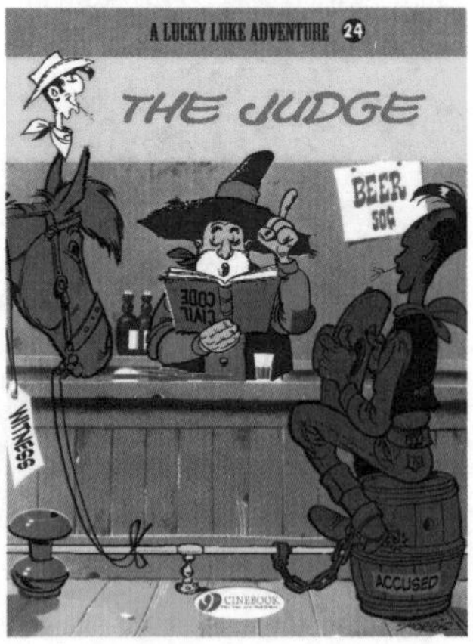
A LUCKY LUKE ADVENTURE 24
THE JUDGE
BEER 50¢
ACCUSED

COMING SOON

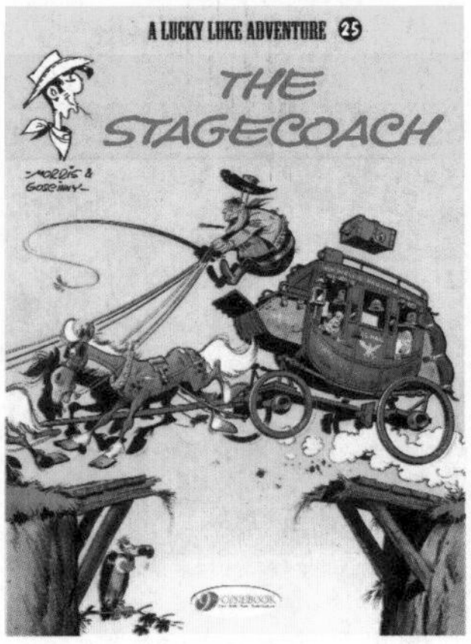
A LUCKY LUKE ADVENTURE 25
THE STAGECOACH
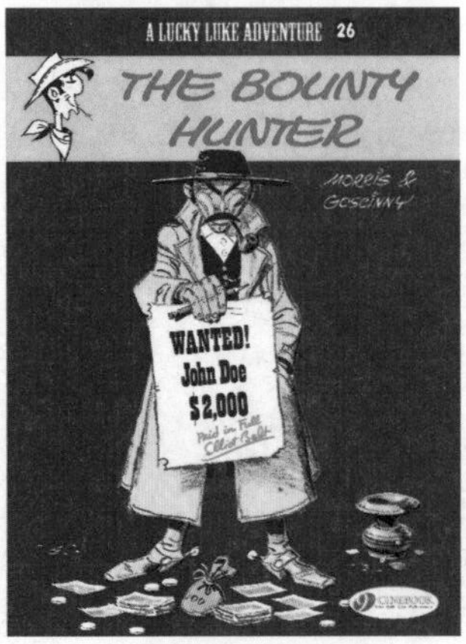
A LUCKY LUKE ADVENTURE 26
THE BOUNTY HUNTER
WANTED!
John Doe
$2,000
DECEMBER 2010

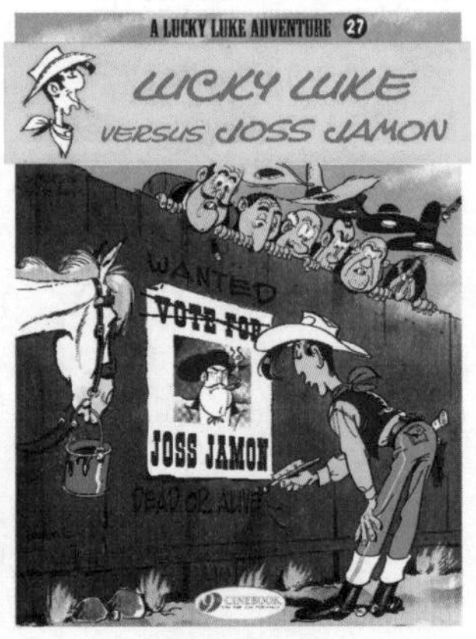
A LUCKY LUKE ADVENTURE 27
LUCKY LUKE VERSUS JOSS JAMON
WANTED
JOSS JAMON
FEBRUARY 2011

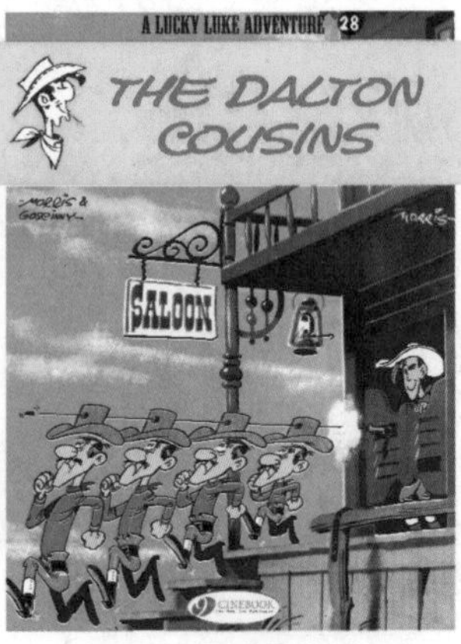
A LUCKY LUKE ADVENTURE 28
THE DALTON COUSINS
SALOON
APRIL 2011